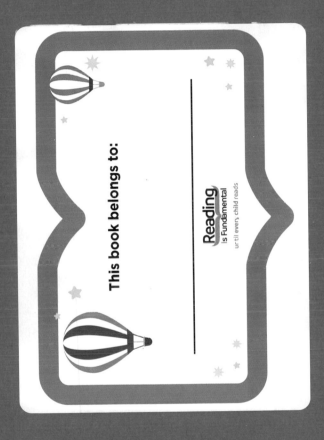

This book belongs to:

Reading
is Fundamental
ur til every child reads

THE SHEPHERD'S
GRANDDAUGHTER

THE SHEPHERD'S
GRANDDAUGHTER

ANNE LAUREL CARTER

GROUNDWOOD BOOKS

HOUSE OF ANANSI PRESS

Groundwood Books / House of Anansi Press
110 Spadina Avenue, Suite 801, Toronto, Ontario M5V 2K4
or c/o Publishers Group West
1700 Fourth Street, Berkeley, CA 94710

We acknowledge for their financial support of our publishing
program the Canada Council for the Arts, the Government of Canada through
the Book Publishing Industry Development Program (BPIDP) and
the Ontario Arts Council.

ONTARIO ARTS COUNCIL
CONSEIL DES ARTS DE L'ONTARIO

Library and Archives Canada Cataloguing in Publication
Carter, Anne Laurel
The shepherd's granddaughter / Anne Laurel Carter.
ISBN-13: 978-0-88899-902-3 (bound).–ISBN-13: 978-0-88899-903-0 (pbk.)
ISBN-10: 0-88899-902-X (bound).–ISBN-10: 0-88899-903-8 (pbk.)
1. Wolves–Juvenile fiction. I. Title.
PS8555.A7727S54 2008   jC813'.54   C2008-902516-4

Cover photograph: Sophie Elbaz/Sygma/Corbis
Design by Michael Solomon
Printed and bound in Canada

Acknowledgments

This novel is a fictional rendering of a complex situation. There are many people to thank. Jehan Helou who invited me to visit Ramallah. The good people of Tamer Institute who love children and books and shared their stories with me. Alia, one of my gracious hosts, whose spirit breathes in the character of Amani. Reema who loves her village and the olive harvest. Atta, a proud farmer whose home has been demolished twice, and who wants to support his family on his land. Dahlia who misses her olive trees. Yusra from Aboud, a village with a long history of tolerance, who dreads the completion of the Separation Wall. Sameh, so smart about "stick to the story." Christian Peacemakers Teams. Writing friends in Toronto, Jerusalem and Ramallah.

I would like to thank the Canada Council for the Arts and the Ontario Arts Council. Support from a jury of my peers gave me the means and confidence to visit the West Bank several times and to devote myself to this story for more than three years.

I want to thank my husband and children for their patience and support, especially my eldest, David, who studied the Middle East and conflict resolution at McGill University and debated with me as I was writing. Thank you for accompanying me on my last research trip. How wonderful to make new friends together.

It has been a privilege to work with my publisher, Patsy Aldana, and my editor, Shelley Tanaka. Thank you for your intelligent, strong vision for the novel.

Out beyond ideas of wrongdoing and rightdoing,
there is a field. I will meet you there.
–Jalal ad-Din Rumi

ONE

THE FIRST DAY AMANI GRAZED SHEEP on her grandfather's mountaintop was nearly her last.

Mama had warned it was too dangerous for a girl who was only six. But Amani's grandfather, Seedo, was a shepherd, and Amani was determined to be one, too. That morning, Allah had answered her prayer. Seedo had taken her with him up the mountain.

For more than a thousand years there had been a shepherd in Amani's family, a son who herded sheep over the low mountains while others farmed the narrow valley below. Along the base of the slopes hardy olive trees grew on stone terraces, but water had to be piped from a highland spring for vegetables and vineyards to survive in the dry valley bed.

After breakfast, Seedo herded his flock up through his olive grove to the top of a small hill. Here, on the oasis, he opened a spigot between two irrigation pipes. He filled the long trough, a bowl for his sheep dog, and a cup for Amani and himself. Before they drank he washed his right hand, then left, praising Allah. *"Bism Allah al-rahman al- raheem."*

11

Now they were ready to climb the steep upper face to the peak.

Trailing behind her grandfather, panting for breath, Amani arrived at the top of the switchbacking path. She glanced back and gasped. Far below, the water trough was as small as her father's new cellphone. From Seedo's Peak the green leaves of the vineyards flowed into each other like water.

And there, on the other side of the valley — that tiny white box perched above the vineyards on the opposite slope. Was that her house? What about the creature moving in and out? It was waving something.

It was Mama, shaking a rug.

Amani's head spun. From the top of the world Mama looked like an ant.

Amani turned away to make the dizziness stop. She took her first steps across Seedo's Peak under the open sky. Saltbush shrubs and tumble thistle grew around the rocks. A hundred sheep rushed past her to eat.

"A shepherd's job is to protect his flock," Seedo said.

Amani's grandfather leaned on his crook, watching her. His strong voice carried over the drone of hungry animals. Nearly seventy years of Mediterranean sun had weathered his skin so that standing there, he reminded Amani of an olive tree.

Amani nodded.

"They're simple animals," he continued. "A shepherd must keep an eye out. This south-east corner is where trouble usually happens."

On one side of the corner was a sheer cliff. One careless step and a sheep, or a girl, would tumble to her death on the rocks below. On the other side of the corner was the path home.

"Your job is to help me watch that path when we come back to the peak," Seedo said. "Can you do that?"

"Yes," Amani said. Why such an easy job? A job for a baby. Then she remembered what her aunt and her six cousins feared most on the mountains.

"What am I watching for? A wolf?"

Seedo laughed, a fan of wrinkles hiding his eyes. "There are no wolves left in these hills. Before your father was born, the villagers feared and killed them. And since 1967 it's been the occupation, driving them off the land."

He stared at her in an odd way. "Most of them, anyway."

Amani said nothing. Was there a wolf or not?

"But that's a story," Seedo said. "And stories are best told when the day is over. I want you to watch for a wayward sheep. Especially the big ram, Nasty. This afternoon he'll be thirsty and try to head for the oasis. They don't go back down the path until the shepherd says it's time."

In the distance, the call to prayer from the village

mosque made Seedo point to the valley. "Do you see how our fields are like a prayer mat to Allah? It's time to pray."

He knelt on the ground, facing south-east. "Prepare your heart to worship Allah. Sweep out anger the way Sitti sweeps dirt from her kitchen."

What was there to be angry about? Around them the sheep bleated, heads nodding as they cropped a bit of grass. Hyssop sweetened the air, and Amani prayed.

All morning they let the sheep graze slowly down the north side of Seedo's mountain that gently sloped into the next valley. In the distance Amani saw the tent wrappings of a Bedouin camp, bright colors of laundry hung out to dry, white goats grazing under small trees.

When they returned to Seedo's Peak Amani remembered her job. All afternoon she watched the path. But none of the sheep went near trouble, thanks to Sahem. Barking like a general, he kept the animals wherever Seedo wanted them.

Nothing went wrong until Seedo said it was time to go home. Amani was sitting on a rock beside her grandfather, listening to the mothers call their lambs, when Seedo stood. His eyes searched the flock.

"The pregnant yearling is missing."

Amani leapt to her feet. "What can we do? Don't we have to go home?"

"When a sheep is missing, the shepherd doesn't leave until it's found. Did one go near the path?"

Amani shook her head. "No, Seedo. I watched."

Seedo's eyes kept searching. "Then she's up here somewhere. She's found a quiet spot to give birth."

Amani climbed onto the rock and shaded her eyes from the bright sun. Around her, a hundred woolly backs had become a sea of white.

What if the ewe had fallen over the cliff? Amani felt a twinge of guilt. She'd watched the top of the path, but once — maybe a few times? — she had to watch Sahem. The sheepdog made her laugh. He was a small brown fence on legs.

Amani listened to the bleating. Beyond the white backs, near the south-east corner, she heard a strange call that sounded like a troubled grunt.

"That way, Seedo!" Amani cried, pointing.

Seedo ran faster than Amani, his kufiyyi billowing behind his head. In front of the cliff, the yearling lay on her side. She'd cleared a hollow nesting spot with her front hoofs.

At their approach she struggled to stand, arching her back. A red balloon of fluid hung from her rear end. She lay down again and the bag burst, soaking the ground.

Seedo crouched by her, crooning, "Easy. There's a beautiful girl. Your baby's coming and we're here to help."

Amani knelt on the other side, glowing. Seedo had said *we*.

The mother's head strained forward, eyes huge as she pushed. A furry wet nose emerged from the swollen pink opening under her tail. Amani had seen other lambs emerge from their mothers in the sheep pen, but here under the open sky, it filled her with wonder.

"Not the head, *Lasamahallah*," Seedo said. "We want the tips of the baby's feet first."

Seedo put his large hand on the wet nose and pushed it back inside, his arm disappearing into the birth canal.

"There's a good mother. I'm pushing gently, careful not to tear anything." Seedo said. Amani memorized everything he did and said. "I'm looking for the lamb's front foot. I've found one. Now I go back for the other. Here they both are, see!"

In Seedo's calloused fingers lay the white tips of two tiny hoofs.

Amani wanted to help, and just as she wished it, Seedo said, "You hold one, and pull gently when I say."

The mother pushed. Amani pulled gently. A shiny black hoof attached to a skinny leg emerged, the furry nose again, a blue tongue lolling to one side, ears flat against the head.

Amani let go, moving out of the way. "The baby's coming! It's coming!"

A long neck and shoulders appeared. Another push and

the whole lamb slipped out, a small ocean of fluid with it. The thin umbilical cord was already broken. The back end of the lamb remained inside a yellowish sac.

The baby didn't move. Amani waited, knowing the mother should start to lick her lamb to life. But the ewe turned away from the wet bundle and scrambled to her feet.

"What's wrong?" Amani cried. "Why isn't she helping her baby?"

"It's her first time. She's shocked by it," Seedo said, his long fingers clearing slime from the lamb's mouth and nose. "If the mother doesn't lick, the shepherd has to make sure the baby doesn't suffocate."

The lamb coughed, taking its first breath. Legs kicked, tearing free from the sac. Free of her burden, the new mother jumped sideways and bounded away.

"Oh, no, you don't," Seedo cried, leaping to his feet.

Amani stayed beside the wet lambkin. It struggled to stand, legs splayed. Amani tugged it around the middle, pulling and pushing until it stood, blinking and uncertain.

Only a few steps away the cliff dropped, sharp and sheer. Amani noticed it, and was glad the lamb was weak and wobbly.

"Ahlan," Amani said, hugging it around the shoulders.

When she pulled away, the worst thing happened. The lamb took one step, then another, toward the cliff. Amani

17

moved quickly, putting herself between the lamb and death, her heels backing toward the crumbling lip of the precipice behind her.

"Aiee! Not this way! Go back to your mother!"

"Stop, little shepherd," Seedo called, dragging the ewe toward them. He was eyeing Amani strangely.

"Take a step toward me, Amani. Another step. That's it. Bring her here. She needs to find milk. And the mother needs to teach her baby the sound of her voice."

Amani obeyed her grandfather's instructions. His face and voice relaxed when she finally stood beside him. He helped the lamb bunt its head hard into the ewe's pink udder, already swollen with milk. Seedo removed the waxy plug from a teat and the baby latched on, sucking greedily.

Seedo raised his head quickly to check the flock. Amani did, too.

Nasty was heading for the path.

Seedo grumbled, "That ram will be in the barbecue pit if he doesn't behave. Thinks he'll sneak down to the oasis while I'm busy."

"I'll stop him!" Amani cried.

"Not today you won't. Leave him to Sahem." Seedo's voice was firm. "You need to be bigger and carry a shepherd's crook before you tell a ram what to do."

Distracted by their talking, the ewe tried to escape

again. Seedo held her fast so the lamb could resume feeding, his back to Amani, Sahem and the ram.

Nasty barreled toward the path and the drink he wanted. Where was Sahem? The sheepdog was chasing another ewe, running the other way.

Amani had to act now. She grabbed Seedo's wooden crook where he'd dropped it on the ground.

Nearing the top of the path the big ram slowed. He was three times bigger than Amani. His eyes were two black slots of meanness below the daggers of his curling horns.

"Aiee!" Amani yelled, charging at him, dragging Seedo's crook, too heavy to lift. "*Rouh!* Not that way!"

The ram took a step sideways, lowered his massive head and sent Amani flying.

TWO

TOSSED LIKE A SACK OF OLIVES, Amani landed beside the cliff. Her chest hurt. Her arm stung where Nasty's horn had scraped her skin.

Amani glanced at her fingers, shocked to see red. She wiped them on her shirt, only to regret it.

If Mama saw blood, a girl only six would be staying home tomorrow.

In a rage, Amani rolled forward and charged Nasty again.

Two familiar hands scooped her — a ball of flailing limbs and fists — off her feet. Seedo set her on the ground, well away from the edge of the cliff, hands gripping her shoulders.

"Take a breath, Amani. Listen to me. Calm down."

He examined her face and arm, waiting for her attention.

"You remind me of myself when I was a boy. You'll be a shepherd one day but you have much to learn. Are you willing to learn?"

Amani tried to nod, her thoughts still attacking Nasty.

"Don't run at him. You show an animal, especially a

ram, the way you want him to go. Guide him there with your arms, your voice and, especially, Amani, your spirit. It's your spirit that talks to him."

Amani stopped squirming.

"Here. Take this small stick in your right hand, and I'll use my big one. Give him his dignity. Let him think he is choosing his path. Imagine a gate with your left hand, and show him the safe path you want him to take."

They moved together like Mama's two hands when she played her piano. Nasty huffed and shook his ornery head. But he didn't turn away. Seedo stood behind Amani, one hand firmly on her wrist, reminding her to open the gate of her uphill arm while the stick in her downhill hand stayed beside Seedo's crook, blocking the steep path that led to water and home.

Not that way, their sticks ordered.

This way, their gates and spirit voices urged. *Up.*

Nasty leapt through the gates and joined the flock.

"Now," Seedo said. "It's time to go home."

He picked up the new lamb and carried it down the rugged path while Sahem brought the rest of the flock behind Amani.

By the water trough, Seedo set the lamb on the ground and pointed east with his crook.

"I promised you a story. Do you know what lies that way?"

Amani stared east. Her grandfather's mountain had two peaks—the large flat one where they'd just grazed the sheep and, separated by a gully, a rocky spire that rose like a tower over the oasis.

"The Camel's Hump?"

"I mean beyond it," Seedo said.

No one explored beyond the Camel's Hump. Not even her ten-year-old brother, Omar, went up there.

A stone retaining wall ran along the base of the Camel's Hump. Above it, the slope was a pile of large boulders. It was a perfect place to twist an ankle or meet a snake.

Seedo opened the spigot. He performed his ablutions, washing his right, then left hand, and thanking Allah.

"Before our ancestors built that wall, any shepherd who went up there never came back."

The sheep were pushing and shoving to find a place to drink.

"Because there's no water?"

"No. Because it was the wolf's territory."

Amani whispered, "Amma Fatima says wolves used to eat children who wandered away from home."

Seedo took his time answering. "Like everyone else, she was taught to fear them. Amma Fatima's wrong. They don't eat humans."

"They eat sheep!"

"So do we. Wolves eat the weak and the old from a flock. It's the way Allah created the world."

Amani stopped listening. At the end of the oasis she saw the trees in the top row of the olive terraces. Through the orchard past the sheep pen was Seedo's house. Which meant Mama wasn't far.

Amani held out her bloodied arm and hands.

"What's wrong?" Seedo asked.

"Remember what you promised Mama?" Amani wailed.

Every morning, *kul yom*, Amani asked Mama's permission to tend the sheep.

"Mama? Can I go with Seedo today?"

"Kul yom," Mama would sigh, shaking her head. *"Kul yom* you ask me. *Kul yom* I have the same answer. Chasing sheep on a mountaintop is too dangerous for a girl. You're only six. No. You'll be safer with me at home."

This morning, on the steps to Seedo's porch, her brother had lined up with their cousins for shekels to buy treats in the nearby village. Her cousin Wardeh had wagged a know-it-all finger at Amani. Three years older than Amani, Wardeh had grown up bossed around by five older sisters. She loved doing the same to Amani.

"You'll learn when you go to school, Amani," Wardeh said. "Girls can not be shepherds. When summer's over you'll forget all about those stupid sheep."

23

"Never! I'm going to be a shepherd!" Amani shouted. "Today!"

Only one person in the world understood. Seedo. He was already in the garden, on his way to the pen. Seedo never interfered in family squabbles. When his sons argued, Seedo turned off his hearing aid.

Amani jumped off the porch and chased after Seedo. She yanked his long robe to get his attention.

"Can I come with you today? Please, Seedo?"

His eyebrows rose.

"I want to be a shepherd," she cried. "Wardeh says I can't because I'm a girl."

Seedo frowned as he thought about this.

"Are you strong enough to climb by yourself?" he asked. "I'm too old to carry you."

"Yes!"

He held out his free hand.

Mama yelled from the porch, "No! She'll get hurt!"

Amani had grabbed what she could — several fingers of her grandfather's extended hand. Would he change his mind?

"I promise you, Rose, nothing will harm her. I'll return her safely, or you can keep her home until she's older."

Now Amani repeated Seedo's promise while the sheep drank beside them at the trough. She stretched out her bloody shirt, trying not to cry.

24

"Mama won't let me tend the sheep again if she sees blood."

"Hmm," Seedo said, examining her carefully. "Then we'd best clean you up."

Seedo washed Amani's arm and hands, removing all the blood that had dribbled and dried before gently sponging the wound.

"It's not deep," he said. "It will scab over and disappear in a few days. Give me a little time to think about the problem of your shirt."

He whistled for Sahem and herded the sheep down through the olive terraces and into the pen. Amani dragged behind. Any second now she'd meet Mama. Mama would see her shirt and the red scrape on her arm.

But they didn't run into Mama. They met Sitti, Amani's grandmother. She was taking dry laundry off a line in the yard and hanging up wet.

"Where's Rose?" Seedo asked her quietly.

Eight tomatoes sat on a broken stool beside the basket of dry clothes.

Sitti's memory was bad. The family had a system of leaving clues to help her remember their comings and goings. Sitti stared at the fruit.

"Rose is with Fatima and our six granddaughters. They went to pick tomatoes in the greenhouse."

"I learned something today about our seventh granddaughter. Amani takes after me. Amani was born to be a shepherd."

Amani swung wildly between fear and hope. "What about Mama?"

Seedo put a finger to his lips. "What was my promise? To return you safely. And I did."

Sitti tutted. "A fine pair you are. Born like sheep on the mountain. Find her something clean to wear."

Seedo pulled a long-sleeved shirt off the line and Amani changed into it happily.

"I'll clean this blood stain right now," Sitti said. "No one will ever know."

And no one did.

THREE

THE LAST DAY OF SUMMER HOLIDAYS arrived like a bee sting.

At breakfast, Amma Fatima smiled at Amani, holding out Wardeh's faded blue-and-white school uniform.

Amani lowered her head, refusing to meet Amma Fatima's eyes. She'd been so sure summer would last forever.

"Come, Amani. Try it on," her aunt coaxed, her voice like honey. "I'll alter it for you so it fits."

Amani stood and held out her arms.

"See, Sheep Girl?" Wardeh whispered in her ear. "You have to go to school."

Amani stiffened, trying not to let her cousin's uniform touch her skin.

More bee stings followed the fitting. Seedo had a headache and told Omar to climb the mountain with them. In the olive orchard Seedo stopped in the upper terrace and sat on a low bench circling the wide trunk of a thousand-year-old tree.

"I'll rest here a while," Seedo said. "The light hurts my eyes. Omar will go with you."

What was Seedo thinking? Omar loved science, not sheep. What if Omar tried to boss her or the sheep around?

But Omar just sat on the stone wall, reading a book about electricity. He would have sat there all day if Sahem hadn't barked at him to move.

On the summit Amani wandered away with the sheep. The second call to prayer rang out from the mosque in the village.

Allahu Akbar, the enormous voice of the muezzin sang. God is great.

Amani headed back to her brother.

"Omar, is the muezzin a giant?"

Omar threw back his head, howling with laughter. "The muezzin's a man, you ninny."

"But his voice is so huge."

"It's loudspeakers," he said, still laughing. "On the roof of the mosque sending out sound waves."

"Sound waves?" Amani repeated, irritated. She hated when he called her ninny.

"Sound," Omar lectured eagerly, "is a series of compression waves moving through air. They travel over three hundred meters a second."

She splashed her hand through the nothing air. "Where? There aren't any waves."

Omar snapped his book shut. He wagged his finger at

her. "Here are the facts, so listen. The muezzin's a man. He sings the call to prayer five times a day into a loudspeaker. His voice carries down the valley on sound waves. It's a good thing you're going to school tomorrow. If you spend any more time with sheep you'll be just as stupid as they are."

At this Amani burst into tears. She fled down the slope, across the oasis and into the upper terraces of olive trees.

"Something wrong, Amani?"

Seedo sat on the shaded bench, watching her. He held out his hand.

She wiped her eyes. Head hung low, she approached her grandfather, stopping when Seedo's dusty feet were in front of hers.

Seedo tapped the tips of his sandals together — his way of saying hello when Amani wouldn't look at an adult.

"Sit with me, Amani."

She crawled into his arms.

"What happened?"

"Omar…"

Seedo rocked her gently. "I grew up with brothers, too. We were always fighting, though not quite as bad as your father and uncle. When you get to be my age it's a blessing to wear a hearing aid. At least you can turn it off."

Amani wiped her dribbly nose.

"Can you smell the olives?" Seedo said.

29

She nodded.

"The best fragrance in Palestine. Better than Fatima's roses, but don't tell her I said that."

Amani burrowed her head into her grandfather's shoulder. Other smells — olive oil soap, wood smoke from Sitti's bake oven, and the homespun wool of his cloak — mixed together. Seedo's smell.

"I never want to go to school."

He stopped rocking. "Don't you want to be smart like Omar?"

She shook her head. "I want to be a shepherd. Like you."

His arms tensed around her. "You're a girl. One day your uncle will decide things for the family. He doesn't understand wanting to be a shepherd."

But Seedo understood. It sounded like maybe.

"I'm not saying yes, Amani. Or no. Give me a little time to think about it."

That evening the family gathered on Seedo's porch for an early supper. Even though her uncle's house was right beside Seedo's, her cousins were the last to arrive, chattering about school.

Amani eyed her grandfather. Which path would she take tomorrow? One with him, tending their sheep? Or the one above her house on the opposite side of the valley — the path her cousins and brother took to school.

Seedo prayed *Bism Allah*, and they began to eat.

Everyone was hungry, and the meal was a silent one until Mama suddenly said, "Amani's shepherding is over. School starts tomorrow."

"She's not going," Seedo said quietly.

Everyone stopped dipping into the bowls of steaming vegetables on the low table. Amani stared at Seedo, then Mama, wondering if her mother would say something, but it was Ammo Hani, as Seedo's eldest son, who spoke.

"All the children go to school."

"I'm getting old. Amani might take over as shepherd one day. I want to train her as my apprentice."

"Palestinians have no future as shepherds." Ammo Hani's face turned red.

Baba looked equally upset. "How will Amani get a good job without an education?" he asked. "I want her to go to school like Omar."

Mama and Amma Fatima nodded. "Like her cousins. All the girls from the village go to — "

"I've made my decision," Seedo said. "Aref and Rose, you can teach her to read and write in the evenings. Omar, you can teach her math and science. Amani learns quickly. If you teach her well she won't fall behind the other children."

Amani wanted to crow like their rooster. Seedo was the head of the family. All the adults obeyed him, even her uncle, though his eyes argued the whole time he sipped his coffee.

After supper Wardeh suggested a game of ghummayeh in the vineyard. Amani sped past her cousins, down Seedo's driveway and onto the tractor path that crossed the valley toward her house. On both sides of her, a canopy of green leaves covered the tall vines. Ripening grapes hung in the shadows. It was her favorite place to hide from her cousins.

To Amani's disappointment they only played one game. The girls were worried about getting their uniforms ready, and headed home.

Walking with Omar, Amani picked up a stone. Ahead, their house was identical to their grandfather's and uncle's. White. One story. With a concrete block exterior. The only difference was that their house had no porch.

Omar gave her a sideways look.

"I could teach you some science if you find more stones. Different sizes."

Since their fight, he'd been extra nice. And since it felt like a game, Amani decided to cooperate. With her pockets full of stones, she followed Omar to the well beside Mama's vegetable gardens.

"Line them up from biggest to smallest. This is an experiment."

"What's that?"

"Something a scientist does. You start with a question, make observations, and figure out a conclusion."

"Okay. What's the question?"

"Understanding waves. Drop your stones, starting with the biggest, into the well and tell me everything you observe."

The big stone plunked and disappeared below the surface. Big dark circles spread over the water.

Amani dropped another stone, and another.

"The waves are getting smaller."

Omar beamed at her. "What's making the waves get smaller?"

"The rocks. As the rock gets smaller, the waves get smaller."

Omar clapped. "See? You're a good scientist."

Amani didn't see what Omar loved so much about science. But because it made him happy, she dropped the rest of the stones and repeated her conclusion. The lighter the stone, the faster the waves disappeared.

She did not tell him that Seedo's comments at supper were rippling back into her thoughts.

What had Seedo meant about growing old? And her taking over one day? Was he going to die? It was too terrible to imagine.

Amani took the last tiny stone, small as a lentil, and imagined it held the terrible thought. She dropped it into the well.

Not a trace of the stone remained, not the slightest wave.

FOUR

A YEAR PASSED. Amani's eldest cousin, Nahla, graduated from high school. A young man arrived from Al Khalil to ask Seedo's permission to marry her. Summer ended with a week of wedding celebrations and Nahla leaving to live with her husband's family.

The night before school started, they were thirteen eating supper on Seedo's porch. Before coffee, Ammo Hani pointed a finger at Amani.

"School would be good for you. Don't you want your life to turn out as well as Nahla's? See how a good Muslim daughter behaves!"

"You want me to go to school to get married?"

He sputtered like a balloon losing air. "No! I want you to learn obedience. Running after sheep is not becoming in a girl. No one will want to marry you."

Mama stopped eating. "A girl dreams of many things, not only marriage."

"*Khalas,*" Seedo said. "As long as I'm alive, Amani is my apprentice."

Ammo Hani persisted. "And after you're gone? We won't keep sheep in the future."

Seedo laughed. "Why not? Are you planning to give up meat?"

"We need to focus our energy on our crops and fighting the occupation."

"How many occupations has Palestine known? The Israelis will give up and leave our land eventually."

"Not this time. Israel lets settlers take over Arab buildings in Al Khalil and sends soldiers to defend them. They've closed Shuhada Street. Put up more checkpoints. Every year it gets more dangerous in the old city. Shops are closed. Many are leaving. We can't take the children with the harvests this fall."

Not take them into Al Khalil? How could Ammo Hani say such a thing? Even Sitti loved to climb into the back of the truck at harvest time. It was fun to shop in the bustling outdoor market and visit their relatives. After they took the olives to be pressed into oil, they ate pizza in a restaurant and stayed up half the night.

And if the helmeted soldiers pointed their rifles at them? Amani clutched Mama's hand and imitated the adults. Never move suddenly. Obey the soldiers. Wait quietly on the sidewalk until they say you can move.

"That's the city," Seedo said, shrugging.

Ammo Hani shook his fist. "It's coming here, too. The Israelis just confiscated the valley north of us. How will you graze a large flock of sheep if they take away your pastureland?"

This Amani understood. Earlier in the day, Seedo had stopped her from leading the sheep down the north slope of the mountain. "We can't go down there anymore," he'd said grimly. "The Israelis have declared it a security zone."

She'd looked east to the Bedouin camp. No tent wrappings. No colorful lines of laundry. No animals under the acacia trees. The Bedouin were gone.

In front of her uncle, Seedo hid the sadness Amani had seen all day.

"I still have my mountain and the valley." A smile lifted the corners of his eyes. "You've pestered me for years to slow down. It's a good time to sell twenty or so from the flock. You and Aref can use the money to build that new greenhouse you want so badly."

One happy year followed the next like sheep on the path to Seedo's Peak. Amani's cousins graduated from high school until only Wardeh remained at home. Wardeh's nickname for Amani unfortunately spread into the village. Sheep Girl became excluded from games and conversation. But Amani didn't care. She was learning how to midwife a difficult delivery and care for the flock with her grandfather.

One spring night when she was twelve, a lamb became infested with maggots and died in the pen. Amani and Seedo stood together at the gate, looking at the dead body covered in flies, while the mother bawled beside it.

"Go ask your father or Hani to help me remove it from the pen," Seedo said.

Amani knew it was important to do this quickly to prevent the spread of disease. She hestitated. The thought of touching the stiff, dead body made her queasy.

Seedo waited, then said quietly, "Sheep grieve their dead just like we do. A good shepherd respects that and helps them get over their loss."

Amani listened to the bleating inside the pen. The other sheep were upset. Several had surrounded the lamb's mother, trying to console her.

"Give me the extra gloves," Amani said. "I can do it."

FIVE

AMANI'S THIRTEENTH SUMMER was marked by three important changes. The first was in her body. For months Wardeh acted as if she had a right to ask, "Did you get your period yet?" Her tone guaranteed advice if Amani nodded. Which was why Amani was pleased that she could finally say yes when Wardeh asked for the last time. "Mama showed me what to do. Do you want to know about estrus in a sheep?"

No. Wardeh did not.

Much more exciting to Amani was her search for a veterinarian. Seedo had reduced the flock to seventy and the remaining animals were especially precious to Amani.

"Are there any books at school about how to care for sheep?" she asked her brother.

"I'll ask Miss Aboushi. Have you tried finding a vet?"

Seedo raised his eyebrows. "A vet? What could a stranger tell me about my sheep?"

The book her brother brought home from Miss Aboushi gave Amani new ideas. She read aloud to him bits about rotating the flock's pastureland and how all the animals in the valley needed to be innoculated against contagious diseases. Omar nodded, impressed.

So when Baba had to go into the city for a meeting, Omar persuaded him to drop them off at an internet café near the eastern gate. "It's nowhere near Shuhada Street. I'll keep her safe."

Omar helped Amani find and email a government veterinarian. When the vet discovered her age, and that she was interested in breeding a strong flock, he agreed to visit in the fall. And would the youngest shepherd in Palestine like to be part of an experiment? YES, Amani answered. Good. The vet would bring a surprise.

Amani was so immersed in her plans that she didn't notice when the third change began. That change was in Seedo. All she noticed was the first morning Seedo sat on the bench around the ancient olive tree.

It was August. Hot. At night the valley held the day's sweltering heat and Amani's family joined her uncle's to sleep out with their grandparents on their wide porch. Last night everyone had tossed restless, sleepless, hoping for a breeze.

"Take the sheep up to graze by yourself, Amani," Seedo said, waving her on.

"Do you have a headache?"

"No. I'm tired. Don't fuss."

But the next day Seedo sat on the bench again, and

39

every day after that. The sun hurt his eyes. The climb was too long. Amani suggested rotating the flock's pastureland. The peak needed a rest. Seedo nodded. Fine. Amani could take the sheep anywhere she liked. He wanted to rest in the shade of his olive grove.

The night before school started, Amani was helping her aunt bring coffee from the kitchen when her uncle said something that made her tighten her grip on the tray.

"The Israelis are starting to build a new settlers' highway. It looks like it's heading for our valley. If it does, it will cut through the heart of everyone's fields."

Puddles of black coffee spilled onto the tray.

"How can they build a highway on our land?" Amma Fatima asked, taking charge of the tray. "Isn't it illegal?"

"It's happening all over Palestine. They're building more settlements. No one stops them. It's up to us. We have to fight back before it's too late."

Baba shook his head. "Not with weapons."

Amani's hands trembled. A highway through their fields. Fighting.

Omar sat tense and alert, his eyes shifting from Baba to their uncle with excitement.

Mama put a hand on Baba's arm, but Baba wouldn't be silenced.

"Protesting is a good way of fighting. There are peace-workers in Palestine and Israel, and from the international community, agencies that can help us resist without violence."

"Your way is useless! The Israelis use military force to take what they want. How many villages have to be destroyed before you'll fight with me?" Ammo Hani reached out his hand. Any closer and he'd twist off Baba's ear. "Not my village. Not my fields. I fight weapons with weapons."

Mama clapped her hands. "*Khalas!* Both of you. Can't you see your father's tired? Let him speak."

Seedo held up a weary hand. "Rose is right. Your talk of fighting exhausts me. We continue our lives as always. You cultivate the land. Amani and I tend the sheep."

Ammo Hani was not so easily silenced. "Israel isn't going to let us continue our lives as always. They want our land and water. They'll use any means to take it. Harass us with soldiers, throw us in jail, allow settlers to make our lives so crazy, we'll beg to leave our own homes — "

Seedo cut him off. "I agree with Aref. We'll never have peace through violence. They don't trust us."

"And I don't trust them."

The coffee sat untouched.

"I've seen you resting in the olive orchard," Ammo Hani said suddenly to his father. "You're sick, aren't you?"

"I'm tired, that's all. Wait until you're my age. You'll be resting, too."

"No, Baba." Ammo Hani paused. "What is Amani learning? How to avoid reality like her dying grandfather?"

There was a hush on the porch.

Amani stared at Seedo. Dying? Why did Ammo Hani have to scare them this way?

The answer was obvious. So he could exert his will. So he could run the family his way.

SIX

OLIVES HUNG WASHED BY the fall rains, ready to be picked, when the government vet arrived. Amani was delighted. So was Seedo. A visitor would be a good distraction for the valley. After the argument on the porch, Fatima and Wardeh had gossiped in the village. For two months visitors had filled Seedo's porch.

"Are you in pain?"

"How do you feel today?"

Seedo hated fussing as much as arguing.

Baba and Ammo Hani wanted him to see a doctor at the hospital in Al Khalil, but it was too dangerous. Battles were breaking out on the streets of the city. To complicate the situation, construction of the new settlers' highway had made travel difficult. The Israelis had set concrete blocks across the old road to Al Khalil. Vehicles weren't allowed into the city through the eastern gate. Their only way to an open gate was by a roundabout route over the hills. The villagers had nicknamed it the Road Through Hell.

Baba was on his cellphone constantly. Even Ammo

Hani was grateful when Baba's efforts brought a mobile clinic to the village. A white van with a red crescent on its doors took Seedo's blood samples away for testing.

The vet's arrival distracted Amani from worrying about Seedo. The visitor led his gift into the sheep pen.

"The Romanian breed produces more meat and offspring," he said. "All I ask is that you keep accurate records of her lambs and their progeny every spring."

Amani knelt to admire the small, sturdy sheep with the beautiful black face.

"I'm going to call you Romania," she said, giving her a welcoming hug. Most adult sheep were standoffish with strangers, but Romania kissed Amani's cheek.

"Careful!" the vet warned, watching them over the rails. "That's her favorite trick. She's been spoiled rotten. Next thing you know she'll want a private room in your house, so be strict with her."

Amani didn't care. She hugged Romania again.

Seedo sat on a stool while Amani talked to the vet. She pointed to a lamb scratching himself against a fence post. Under his tail the wool was a glossy, stinky green. Since the heavy rains he'd been grazing the wet valley land and had developed diarrhea. Flies swarmed his bottom even though Amani had sheared the area under his tail.

"He'll be dead soon if you don't get rid of the maggots. Hold him down."

The vet opened his black leather bag while Amani pinned the animal to the ground. The vet poured a bit of medicine down the unhappy lamb's throat.

"Those swarming flies have laid their eggs. Maggots feed on anything they can get their little mouths on. Their bites itch and so he scratches for relief not knowing he's creating fresh cuts. His raw skin only feeds more maggots, making him sicker." The vet hesitated. "You have to clean his infested bottom thoroughly to make sure they don't come back. Can you do it?"

Amani hated the wiggly yellow maggots.

"Yes."

He handed her a pair of steel shears and instructed her how to snip and clip more of the ram's backside. Maggots burrowed deep into the wool trying to escape as she worked.

Amani spoke to the ram gently. "No more maggots for you, *habeebi*."

The vet finally said "enough" when she'd shaved away all the infested wool, exposing a huge circle of pink flesh around a thin white tail.

"Teramicin next," he said, passing her a can. "It stings, so I'll hold him."

The ram bucked with pain while Amani sprayed the bright blue antibacterial medicine with a steady hand.

"The last step kills any remaining eggs and keeps the

flies from coming back for a few days." The vet removed the lid of a plastic tub and held it under Amani's nose.

Amani jerked back, gagging at the sour smell. The vet grinned.

"Exactly what we want those flies to do. Smear it down his rump and back legs. You're a good shepherd, Amani."

Amani sat in the vet's passenger seat and introduced him to the other shepherds in the valley. Everyone welcomed the guest. He innoculated their animals against brucellosis and other contagious diseases. Amani realized the vet knew things about sheep even her grandfather did not.

When the visit was over, Amani helped the vet load his things in his truck. He refused to stay for supper, worried the roads might close.

"Can you visit the valley next spring?"

"Lambing season is overbooked. But I'll try to fit you in. No promises. Email me any questions you like."

In the kitchen at the back of her house, Amani chopped cucumbers into a fresh yogurt salad. Mama took leftover fellafel from the fridge, humming the melody of a new piece she'd been playing on the piano. They carried supper to the windowed room with a view over the vineyards.

They ate as night fell over the valley, cold, damp and quick. Fuel was expensive; the space heater sat unlit in a corner. There were colder nights to come. Mama found them each a warm sweater while Amani cleaned up. They'd have coffee at Seedo's house.

Amani stepped outside. A billion starry ice crystals lit the sky.

Steps behind Omar, Amani ran through the vineyards to keep warm. On the left side of Seedo's driveway, Ammo Hani's house was dark. Light radiated from two windows in Seedo's house.

Amani followed Omar inside, drawn to the sound of the TV in the salon. Her aunt, uncle and Wardeh were in armchairs, focused on the news broadcast. Omar took the comfortable rocking chair. Sitti was curled up, small as a cat, asleep at one end of the long, lumpy sofa. Seedo sat wrapped in a blanket at the other. He nodded at Amani, motioning for her to sit beside him.

Tension filled the room. Even before she looked at the screen, Amani knew the news was bad. All over Palestine people were fed up with the occupation. There were riots and protests where people got shot.

Amani looked at the screen and felt sick. People stood crying on a blood-stained sidewalk by a building with a gaping, blackened hole. Amani's parents sat down just as the announcer repeated the details of a suicide bombing in Israel.

"...late yesterday evening on Ben Yehuda Street..."

Mama groaned. "Jerusalem."

"…at this popular pedestrian mall. Eleven young people aged fourteen to twenty-one died immediately from the two explosions. Twenty minutes later another bomb exploded in a parked car."

Baba was angry. "Innocent children killed, and for what?"

Ammo Hani shouted back, "Because they live in houses and land stolen from us and don't care. They want security for themselves while four million Palestinians remain refugees. They occupy our land and put us in jail. It's a fight for our freedom."

Omar's chair jerked wildly. "The bombers are martyrs."

"Don't talk that way," Baba said harshly. "Where did you learn that? The Qur'an doesn't teach us to kill civilians, innocent people."

Fist raised, Ammo Hani stood. "Innocent? No Israeli is innocent. Why should we let them live in peace? They don't deserve it."

"That's the craziest thing you've ever said, Hani. Every human being deserves to live in peace. That's why they don't trust us." Baba pointed at the weeping mother being interviewed. "How do you know she didn't care about us before? How will she care about us now?"

The screen went blank. Seedo stood beside the TV, his finger retreating from the Power button.

"I'm tired," he said. "It's time for evening prayers. Go home, all of you. Learn to pray."

Mama moved quickly to the door, giving Baba the look. They were going home. Now.

Amani walked with Omar behind her parents, back through the vineyards, listening to Baba's curses. He'd been a fool to argue with Hani.

Mama's voice turned light, teasing. "Aren't you glad our house is on the other side of the valley? Every family needs a little distance. From now on we watch the news at our house."

Before going inside, Amani looked down at the valley. In the moonlight the vineyards flowed like a dark river. Terraces rose in steps along every hillside. Hundreds of olive trees, hundreds of years old, reminded her that they had survived other occupations. They would survive this one, too. *Insha'allah*.

Work on the settlers' highway stopped abruptly the next day. In spite of heavy rain, Amani's parents walked into the village for a meeting. Up the valley, armed Israeli settlers had chased farmers from their orchards and burned several houses. There'd been another suicide bombing in Haifa. Omar tried the TV but the images were fuzzy, like the sound.

"Is it because of the rain?" Amani asked.

"No," he answered. "They've shut off most of our power to punish us. Want to know what happened to Yasser?"

With their parents out, Omar talked freely about his friends in Al Khalil. Many had joined resistance cells to fight in the streets. Two had been caught and taken to prison.

"Someone informed on Yasser. Last night the Shin Bet came looking for him. He's disappeared, gone into hiding."

"Where? Do you know?"

Omar nodded. His eyes shone with excitement.

"One day, if I don't come home from school, tell them I'm fighting the Israelis."

"What about school? Becoming a scientist?"

"Freedom is more important."

Seedo's only living brother, Mundher, arrived the next day from Al Khalil for the olive harvest. He brought the latest news. A curfew had turned the city into a prison. His taxi had been the last allowed out through the checkpoint. Israeli tanks had arrived, their long guns aimed at neighborhoods where Palestinian resistance fighters were hiding. Helicopters buzzed over houses and stores. Israeli army jeeps patrolled the streets, warning over loudspeakers that anyone who opened a door, even a window, would be shot.

When Amani was six she'd learned to watch for trouble in one place: the south-east corner of Seedo's Peak. Now it threatened to come from any direction, even the sky.

SEVEN

AMANI WOKE WITH THE FIRST CALL to prayer. She slipped on warm clothes and ran across the valley to the sheep pen. For the first time in weeks Seedo was there, waiting.

"We need to discuss something before it's too late," he said. "Come."

"Where are we going?"

"To the oasis."

He opened the gate for the sheep. Amani matched her pace to Seedo's slow one, up through the olive trees. Seedo breathed heavily. His feet shuffled forward in small steps. When they emerged from the last row of trees onto the oasis, he collapsed on the low stone wall. His eyes were sunk into his skull like two small caves. His weathered skin held no trace of summer, only winter.

Amani recognized that skeletal look. She'd seen it when an animal neared the end of life. Eyes blurred with tears, she ran to fill the watering trough for the animals.

When she returned, Seedo pointed west.

"Hani's right about this occupation."

"We survived others," Amani said, attempting to be cheerful, the way Mama was with Baba.

"When I was a small boy we had good Jewish neighbors in Al Khalil. These settlers are different. The modern world is different." He shook his head sadly. "Back then we only lived in this valley during spring and summer. We followed the tradition of our ancestors, camping like Bedouin in the cave close to our fields until harvest."

Amani thought of the cave in the hillside behind Sitti's kitchen. They stored equipment there now, and provisions — tea, sugar, flour, pickled vegetables, fruits in syrup, and canisters of olive oil. How wonderful it must have been to sleep in the coolness of its rocky walls.

"I hated going back to the city in the fall," Seedo continued. "I wanted to stay and tend the sheep on these hills. When I was fifteen, the night before our return, my father informed me he'd enrolled me in the best private school in Cairo. He meant to make a businessman out of me. We had a terrible argument. In the middle of the night, I brought the sheep here."

He gestured to the oasis.

"How could I escape my father's plan? I wept in desperation. To my surprise a wolf howled at me."

Amani's mind turned still. Over the years, Seedo had told many stories. Never this one.

"That wolf showed me a path to a hidden meadow, a

place I called the Firdoos. I lived there with the sheep all winter. When I returned in the spring, my father fell to his knees. They'd mourned my death. Not only was I alive, there were more new lambs than ever. My father never questioned my destiny again."

A wolf? A path? A hidden place? Amani's mind ran in several directions. Seedo meant the mountains beyond the Camel's Hump.

Hundreds of thousands of boulders crowded the slope above the stone retaining wall. Amani scanned the slope as she had a thousand times before. There was no path.

"Where, Seedo?"

"It's not for me to show you."

"Why not?"

"It's the wolf's territory."

The flesh rose on the back of Amani's arms. Why would Seedo protect a wolf's territory?

"Did you ever go back?"

"No. I had no need."

Voices called to them from the olive orchard. Baba and Ammo Hani were setting up equipment in the top row of trees.

"The harvest begins," Seedo said. "You know it will be my last. Help me join them."

Baba brought a donkey and helped Seedo pull himself up to ride it, buckets dangling at one side like bells. Omar drove the tractor through the terraces, bringing a wagon loaded with family and food.

Amani herded the sheep up the mountaintop to graze. During the olive harvest Seedo had always left the flock under Sahem's care for a few hours so they could join the harvesters. Amani did, too.

In the upper row of the orchard Baba was perched inside the first tree, picking by hand. On a plastic sheet under it, Seedo sat beside his brother, Mundher, a large man who had once eaten six whole pizzas, a record Omar vowed to beat this year. They were picking leaves from the olives, dropping clean fruit into a bucket between them. The sharp clip of Ammo Hani's pruning shears cut the air.

Amani shimmied out on a branch to pick the fruit hidden under the outer leaves. Seedo's white hair was right below her. She let a few olives fall from her fingers.

"Aii-eee!" Seedo cried, rubbing his head. "There's a monkey in the tree. Mundher, if you stand up, you'll scare it away."

"I'm sending you luck!" Amani cried.

"The only thing I'm standing for is breakfast," Mundher grumbled.

"Who promised you breakfast?" Ammo Hani called, laughing. "We don't have enough."

They had the first tree picked clean before the sun rose.

They lifted the edges of the plastic sheet. Hundreds of dark olives rolled toward the middle, then tipped into a wide funnel atop a waiting bucket.

Cousins and husbands had joined them, all except Nahla who was stuck in Al Khalil with the curfew. The women laid out a feast near the fire where Mama boiled extra eggs in a pot. From a tall silver coffeepot Wardeh poured coffee into tiny cups for everyone. Amma Fatima cooed at the new grandchild she cradled in her arms.

Amani ripped off pieces of Sitti's fresh shrak, dipping into olive oil or red tomatoes, sprinkling dark green za'tar and white salt over each mouthful.

Surrounded by her family under the olive trees, Amani chewed as if she were eating the morning itself.

By the time Amani had the sheep back in the pen and the ewes milked, Seedo was asleep on the porch. Weary relatives were on their way to the village in the wagon. Mama helped Amani carry the pails of milk to Sitti's kitchen at the back of the house. All alone, Sitti sat by the bake oven, holding the big wooden bowl they used to make bread.

"I'm going home to make mamool cookies," Mama said. "Amani?"

Every muscle in Amani's body begged for a rest. "I'll stay with Sitti. Do you want to make bread, Sitti? Shall I get some flour?"

Her grandmother stood, nodding. "That's what I came out here for."

Amani brought a canister from the cave and met Sitti in the kitchen.

"Is it morning?" Sitti asked, measuring ingredients into the bowl.

"No. Almost night."

"Go wake your grandfather on the porch. His memory's getting bad. Have you noticed?"

Amani stirred hard. Flour rose and dusted her sweater white. "He's tired. I'll let him sleep."

Sitti tutted. "If it's not morning, why are we making bread?"

"There won't be time tomorrow. It's the olive harvest. Mundher's visiting. Remember Seedo's brother?"

Sitti laughed, a sign her memory was stirring. "Who could forget Mundher? He eats enough for a village. And he fights with your grandfather. Especially about wolves. Mundher loved to hunt them. Did you know Seedo heard a wolf the night you were born?"

Amani dumped the dough onto a thin layer of flour on the table.

"Tell me the story, Sitti."

"The night you were born there was a curfew. Your mother couldn't get to the hospital." Sitti half sang the story of Amani's birth. "Seedo told her to climb. 'A walk up the mountain is Allah's way of precipitating a birth,' he said. That's where you were born. On the mountain, same as your grandfather, same as the sheep."

Their hands flew, pinching and rolling balls of dough. They piled the balls back into the bowl and Amani hefted it onto her head. The heavy load pressed into her skull bones. Outside, she set it in front of the small, domed bake oven. A concave iron surface, cemented into brick walls, made a skillet roof above red-hot coals inside.

Amani groaned with relief to sit on a stool in front of it.

"You were named Amani for our wishes. Something we give to another to keep safe. Your parents wished you'd grow up in a free Palestine. Seedo wished that you would love Allah. And your brother…"

"Omar," Amani reminded her, gingerly picking off the first browned bread, trying not to burn her finger-tips.

Sitti tossed a fresh circle of dough into the empty place.

"Omar! He wanted you to be a boy."

"And you, Sitti? What did you wish?"

"I wished for a granddaughter who would love to bake shrak with her old grandmother."

Sitti leaned close and kissed Amani's cheek. "Allah was merciful."

By the time the platter was piled high, the family had

returned with fried fish. On the porch Seedo said the prayer and they devoured the evening meal, ending with Mama's date-and-nut-filled cookies.

Mattresses and blankets were laid out. They fell asleep exhausted under the black sky, traces of powdered sugar on their lips.

For three more days, the harvesters picked down the terraces and across the rows of widely spaced trees until every olive was in a sack, and every sack was arranged in neat piles in the back of the old truck.

Amani lay on the ground, too sore to move as the men discussed where to take the olives for pressing.

Baba's phone rang. It was the hospital. The doctors wanted to see Seedo and run a few tests. The curfew in Al Khalil had been lifted for twenty-four hours. Could they bring Seedo in?

"It's a terrible ride," Mundher warned.

"He should go to the hospital," Ammo Hani said. "And we have to take the olives somewhere."

Seedo nodded. "If the olives can make it, so can I."

"I want to go," Omar said.

"Me, too," said Amani, hoping for a happy family ritual, the way it had been when she was younger.

Looks passed among the adults, especially Mama and Amma Fatima.

"May Allah protect us," her aunt said. "Let's all go."

Sitting at the back of the truck, Amani stared into the dark night. The village receded behind them. Ammo Hani turned a sharp left. Humps lay across the old road — the Israeli blockade. The truck bumped slowly on a tractor path across the valley. More sharp turns.

Then, to Amani's surprise, they were on a smooth surface.

Amani leaned out to see where Ammo Hani was driving. They were on the gravel bed of the new settlers' highway.

Suddenly the truck stopped. Doors slammed. Footsteps crunched. Under the moonless sky, sound carried easily.

"…it's on Palestinian land," Amani heard her uncle say. "If we drive on the highway, we'll reach the city in ten minutes."

Baba sounded tense. "If the Israelis catch us they'll take the truck, the olives, and throw us in jail. It doesn't make sense."

Seedo spoke from where he lay bundled in blankets. "Take the Road Through Hell. It may inspire you both to pray to Allah. That would make the trip worthwhile."

At first Amani was relieved. They drove off the settlers' highway. Gentle rocking became violent bouncing. Ammo Hani shifted gears. Amani held on tightly as the truck attacked the slope on the south side of the valley.

They were driving on rough ground. No road at all. The front tires, then back, hit a hole, then a rock. Each time Amani slammed into the wooden rail. Seedo made a small sound every time they jolted. Amani prayed the trip wouldn't last long.

They reached the top of the hill. Across the valley, and west, the electric lights of a settlement shone brightly, illuminating orange tiled rooftops and tall white walls between green treetops. Then they headed downhill, and the settlement disappeared. Amani counted fifteen bumps and started over. Downhill the truck speeded up but the bumping made even her teeth hurt.

The trip went on and on. Amani counted. Up and down more hills until finally, mercifully, the bouncing stopped.

Everyone moaned with relief. They'd reached a road — so smooth, Amani wanted to jump out and kiss it.

The truck slowed. Stopped. Amani heard shouts outside in Hebrew.

"Checkpoint," Omar hissed.

Footsteps. Soldiers appeared at the back of the truck. A blinding light made Amani squint. When her eyes adjusted, she saw rifles pointed at them. Her stomach rammed into her chest. Then she heard Baba saying something in Hebrew before switching to Arabic.

"We're taking my father to the hospital for tests."

Seedo groaned. The light found him where he lay tucked against a sack of olives. Mama knelt beside him, her eyes owling into the light.

The light pounced on Omar. His fist pounded the railing rhythmically, and if eyes could attack, Omar's did.

An order in Arabic. "You! Out!"

There was a flurry of Hebrew while Omar climbed over the rail. Two soldiers grabbed Omar by the arms and led him away. He was gone before Amani could think what to do.

Baba shouted, "Why do you take my son? Where?"

A soldier barricaded his long rifle across Baba's chest. He spoke broken Arabic. "No Palestinian boys in city. We shoot Palestinian boys. He stays at checkpoint until you go home."

"Then I stay with him."

The soldier shrugged and removed his rifle.

Baba and the soldiers disappeared, too. It happened so fast.

"Mama? What do we do now?"

Mama sounded more tired than afraid as the truck started up. "We take Seedo to the hospital. We'll come back to the checkpoint in the morning and hope to pick them up."

At the hospital Seedo was too shaken to walk. A young nurse brought a wheelchair and promised to care for him while they went to the olive press. There was something

61

reassuring about her white uniform and the way she tucked a blanket around Seedo before wheeling him into the big building.

They drove through the crowded streets of the city. People were out shopping, preparing for the next curfew. How Ammo Hani found the unmarked building was a mystery to Amani. Suddenly, there it was. A huge rectangle of light angled onto the cobbled street from the open doorway. A corrugated metal door lay under the ceiling on tracks, above the noisy machines. On the sidewalk adults greeted each other like family. They swapped stories and food while the machines washed, crushed and chewed their olives, separating off the golden oil that they could sell or take home in big plastic containers.

Amani helped unload the sacks, missing Baba and Omar. They loved bringing the harvest to the olive press.

Ammo Hani surprised her by slipping some shekels into her hand.

"Stay with Wardeh. Don't go far. They could impose the next curfew any time."

Her cousin headed for their favorite restaurant.

"Want to split a pizza?" Wardeh asked in the doorway. "If Omar were here he'd try to beat Mundher's record. How many do you think he could eat?"

Amani felt like crying, not eating or playing guessing games. Was Omar safe?

Wardeh slipped her arm through hers. "Are you worried the soldiers will hurt him?"

Amani shrugged. Wardeh had never been nice to her.

"Let's pool our money and buy something for him," Wardeh said, pulling her toward a store.

It was easy to agree on a gift. They bought a huge bag of Omar's favorite candy — peanuts covered in crunchy sweet shells.

Back under the spilled light, Amani sat beside Mama against the wall. The hum and thrum of the olive press lulled her to sleep.

The muezzins were singing the first call to prayer by the time they picked up Seedo from the hospital, then Baba and Omar at the checkpoint.

"So? How was your night?" Mama asked, passing Omar a blanket from the back of the truck.

"I'm going to fight them with my friends. You can't stop me."

Amani put the bag of candies into his hands, wishing she had a gift to keep him safe.

63

EIGHT

A WEEK AFTER OLIVE PRESSING, a doctor phoned. Seedo had advanced leukemia. If the curfew lifted again, he could return to the hospital. At most he had a few months to live.

"Another trip on the Road Through Hell?" Seedo laughed. "Are they trying to kill me?"

Sitti reached for his hand. "Stay home. Not the hospital."

There was a quiet look between them.

They dragged an old sofa and blankets onto the porch. Seedo wanted to spend his last days with a view of the olive terraces and the valley. Again they were swarmed with visits from the village, food, talk and advice. Seedo ate little, rarely spoke and slept often.

Amani grazed the sheep on the slope above her house so Seedo could see them. She waved across the valley, and he always waved back. Omar often sat with him, studying. The Israelis had closed the school for security reasons.

On his last evening Seedo opened his eyes and looked steadily at each family member gathered around him.

"Where's my crook?"

Baba gave it to him.

"My grandfather gave me this crook. It's been a family tradition that a son who carries it becomes the shepherd of the family."

A son. Amani's heart sank.

"The world has changed. Give the crook to Amani."

Amani didn't trust her ears. Surely it was her heart, hoping to hear her own name. She looked at Ammo Hani, waiting for him to take the crook. Ammo Hani stared back at her, arms folded across his chest.

Baba took the crook from Seedo and pressed the smooth, rounded end into her hand. The wood felt warm and alive under her fingers, and she knew.

Seedo had given her his crook.

They buried Seedo in the village cemetery, on his side with his head facing Mecca.

Seedo had been ready for his death. Amani wasn't. She missed him constantly. For a month Mama made Amani's favorite meals as if she were sick. Amani picked at the stuffed peppers and roasted eggplants. Amma Fatima baked fig cakes and carried them across the valley. Amani couldn't finish a slice. Baba bought her a new book and she flipped the pages, pretending to read.

Only Omar won a smile, a real one, when he offered to email the vet for her on Miss Aboushi's computer.

It took all evening to compose three words.

"Romania is pregnant."

If they ate supper on Seedo's porch, Amani forced herself to listen to Baba and Ammo Hani argue. They hadn't sold their grapes in the fall because they hadn't been able to transport them anywhere. The harvest hung rotting under the canopies. The Israelis had set up more checkpoints, demanded new permits. Permits were expensive. Driving through hell was hard on the truck. It needed new tires and parts.

Amani was shocked to realize they needed money badly.

Early in March on a Friday, the weather turned springlike. All winter she'd grazed the sheep down the valley or up the south slopes, giving Seedo's Peak a rest. For the first time in months, she drove them up the switchbacking path and let the sheep graze across the summit toward the north edge.

In the valley below, a car sped along a settlers' highway. Amani felt disoriented. What had happened to the north valley? Looking west, a clump of unfamiliar buildings occupied the ridge on the horizon.

When she checked the herd, Romania stood with her back arched, not far away. A lamb slipped out onto the ground behind her. Romania began licking it to life.

The sight of her favorite ewe giving birth brought Amani back to a world that felt familiar.

"If Seedo were here, he'd call you a wonderful mother," Amani said, sinking to the ground beside them.

Romania shifted her stance, pushing again. Soon a twin lay near the first lamb. Romania licked its head until it moved, then turned her attention back to the first-born.

Amani knew that ewes often licked one baby dry before starting on the next. But then Romania arched yet again. Something small slipped out. Amani stared at the wet surprise on the ground. It took a few seconds to realize it was a third lamb, tiny and motionless, wrapped in its caul.

Romania was distracted by her first-born. The shepherd in Amani had to help before the third lamb suffocated. Amani pulled the membrane off the baby's head and cleared the slime from its nose and mouth. The baby coughed and kicked, pure black and beautiful.

"I'll name you Surprise," Amani said. "And I'll keep you. No matter what."

With the start of lambing season, Ammo Hani visited the pen. The sight of her uncle at the gate made Amani knock over the pail of milk at her feet. The way he stared at the lambs told her his purpose.

Amani righted the pail. Her hands shook. Seedo had always picked the animal to be killed or sold.

She leaned her head against the ewe's woolly coat. Maybe Ammo Hani would go away. No. Of course he wouldn't. He couldn't leave without food for the family or a way to raise money. She hated to admit it, but Ammo Hani could easily open the gate and take one without a word. Instead, he was giving her a chance to be the shepherd.

Seedo's voice spoke inside her: *A shepherd provides for the family.*

Her instinct guided her. During the winter, with no money coming in from the grape harvest, Seedo had agreed to sell the old ones, the extra rams, even some of the ewes. The flock had been trimmed to forty. Nasty and the strong females were critical to the flock's survival.

Amani left the milking pen and picked out a ram lamb. She carried him across the pen, lifted him over the gate and into her uncle's waiting arms.

Ammo Hani didn't say a word but there was a glint of something new in her uncle's gaze. Respect. Amani turned her back to him, hiding the tears on her cheeks.

He came often. Amani gave him every ram lamb, except for Surprise, then the weaker females. Once she found a bag of feed left at the gate, but she would not thank him.

Over the next year the family's need for cash grew. The flock dwindled to thirty, then twenty. Forced to choose, Amani kept only females from Romania's line. Israeli surveyors and soldiers appeared in the vineyards. They were marking the route for the next section of their highway.

"Don't graze the sheep down the valley anymore," her uncle said. "Especially east of the vineyards. It's not safe for you alone. When lambing season comes, I'll sell most of the lambs."

Ammo Hani was a man of his word. He left her with a flock of ten.

One morning in June, a week before her fifteenth birthday, Ammo Hani stood at the gate with the Abu Nader, the husband of Fatima's younger sister, Islah. They lived in the village and kept a small flock for their family's needs.

"Abu Nader needs a new ram. We need cash to buy new tires for the truck." His face and tone were almost an apology.

Amani had two rams left: Nasty and Surprise. Surprise was too closely related to the young females she'd kept for her flock.

With Seedo's crook she drove Surprise to the gate. They led the black ram away, and her heart twisted inside her.

NINE

WATER WAS PRECIOUS.

As the flock grew smaller the watering trough became too long and wasteful. In the spring Ammo Hani had rebuilt it. Now it was watertight, but tiny.

The biggest sheep drank first, crowding out a lamb or two who searched, unsuccessfully, for a way in. Amani had to fill the trough twice, using her crook to push Nasty away and make room for a thirsty lamb. She continued her grandfather's habit of rinsing right hand, then left, before she prayed, *Bism Allah al-rahman al-raheem*.

On the steep climb to Seedo's Peak, Black Face was slow on the path ahead, her udder pink and heavy. After all Amani's care in the fall not to let the immature female get pregnant, Nasty had broken into her pen in January. Amani reminded herself to keep a close eye on the young mother.

On the peak Black Face headed for the rocky gully between Seedo's Peak and the Camel's Hump. Sahem drove her back to the flock.

In the west a strange cloud of dust beyond the village

caught Amani's attention. Yellow machines moved in and out of the cloud.

Israeli bulldozers were attacking the valley.

A protest filled the back of her throat. "No!" she howled.

She imagined everyone in the valley watched, too, hating the sight. A huge wave of anger rose from the valley, washing over her.

She turned away, heading across Seedo's Peak for the north side. Below her, Israeli cars whizzed by sporadically. A yellow bulldozer was parked on her side of their highway. That was new. Why was it there? On the other side, but farther west, an exit led to the new settlement on the far ridge. The settlement was a blur of green. She'd heard they had a swimming pool.

Amani checked the sheep.

Eight. Black Face was gone.

Where?

The gully. Amani ran toward it, thinking quickly. The delivery might be long and complicated. She ordered Sahem to take the flock down to the oasis.

The bottom of the gully lay in shadow. Above it the tip of the Camel's Hump was a tower of gold, reflecting the late afternoon light.

Amani waited, listening.

A grunt. Loud. On her right.

"Where are you?" she called, climbing into the rocks. She saw the black face first, then the rest of the sheep's body. She lay between two boulders on her side.

"It's all right, Black Face," Amani said calmly. "I'm coming."

One front hoof of the baby had emerged. Amani breathed a sigh of relief. Not a breech birth. Gently, she reached inside the birth canal to find the other hoof.

"Push, now. There's a good mother. You can do it."

But the nose didn't appear. Black Face was small. The baby's head might be too big to squeeze through easily. Amani prayed the baby wasn't dead already, its head swelling inside the canal from a premature death.

"Push hard," she said, keeping her voice calm.

"This one!" she said, pulling hard. A nose and black head emerged, two enormous ears slicked back. Then the rest of the body covered by the pasty sac. The last contractions expelled more fluid and a dark placenta. Black Face reached around and began to lick her baby.

Amani laughed when the lambkin sputtered to life.

"She's a beautiful lamb, Black Face. Except she's got a giant head."

Both baby and mother struggled to stand in the cramped space between the rocks.

"If Omar were here he'd call that a stupid place to have a baby," Amani scolded. "A good place to break a leg."

Amani lifted the lamb, then Black Face, to where they could climb more freely out of the gully.

Suddenly, from nowhere, Amani had an eerie sensation that she was being watched. Her skin felt cool, the hair on her neck rising.

Then she heard a bark unlike any she'd heard from a dog in the village. She whipped around. Nothing moved in the gully. She scanned the slope of the Camel's Hump. A slight breeze swept the back of her legs. Whatever was watching her was over there, smelling her.

She froze.

A four-legged animal stood across from her. His coloring made him hard to see on Camel's Hump. He looked like a big dog.

No. Not a dog. She'd seen pictures.

It was a wolf. His head, especially his ears, were large for his scrawny body. His long hair was pale, short on the underside. Up his thick chest and around his head the hair was streaked with black.

His gaze was fixed on her. Amani wanted to run, but her feet were rooted to the ground. She tried to remember everything she'd ever read or heard. A wolf had jaws that could rip apart a sheep's leg in a minute. He was fast. He was cunning. He stalked his prey.

What did he want? Her? Black Face? The new lamb? Why was he standing there like that? Did he have a pack, circling behind her somewhere? His ears were up. So was his tail. Alert. Not aggressive yet.

What had Seedo told her about wolves? It was too long ago! She couldn't remember!

Suddenly she had a crazy thought. Give him something. Below her, the placenta from the birth lay on the ground like a piece of raw meat. She picked it up and began to back up and out of the gully.

"We're leaving. Going home," she said loudly, to Black Face as well as to the wolf.

She dangled the placenta.

"This is good food," she shouted. "Better than my sheep. I'm giving it to you." She hurled it into the gully.

The wolf growled, tail straight out and leapt down the slope.

Amani grabbed the lamb and ran for the path, Black Face at her heels. Half-sliding down the switchbacks, she checked constantly to see if the wolf was as fast as her fear.

When she reached the first tree at the end of the oasis, a sweeping glance at the path and up the Camel's Hump let her relax.

No wolf pursued them.

She didn't dare release the lamb. Shoulders aching, she hurried down through the terraces. Now she had another problem.

What would she tell Ammo Hani and Baba? Anything dangerous had to be shared with the family.

But if she said she'd seen a wolf on Seedo's Peak, she knew her days as a shepherd would be over for good.

TEN

EARLY THE NEXT MORNING Amani brought Black Face into the pen so she could watch her milk Romania.

"After breakfast, I'll take you out to graze the whole day. Soon you'll have more milk. That baby of yours will get so big and strong you won't recognize her in the fall."

Amani carried the half-full pail to the kitchen door. Amma Fatima and Mama would make cheese and yogurt later. Sitti stood inside, mixing bread dough at a small table.

"*Keefik,* Sitti? Isn't it a wonderful day!"

"No school today?" Sitti's voice trailed off in confusion.

Amani reached for a piece of dough and rolled a ball. "It's me. Amani. You're thinking of Wardeh. She's gone to school with Omar. He writes his exams today. I milked the sheep and now I help you bake bread like we do every morning. Remember?"

Sitti rubbed her hand over the saggy skin of her face. "Aieee. My memory. What's to become of me?"

Sitti's memory was evaporating like spilled water under a hot summer sun. Wearing her black dress was the only way she remembered that Seedo had died. Events from the distant past seemed to pool deep in her mind. Amani hoped one might flow to the surface this morning.

Balls of dough flew from their hands. Amani carried the heavy bowl on her head and placed it on the ground between two waiting stools.

"Did you ever see a wolf, Sitti?"

Sitti grinned. "That was a day even I do not forget."

Sitti flattened a ball into a circle and tossed it onto the skillet roof of the bake oven.

"Your grandfather and I were cousins. My parents often came from the city to picnic here in front of the cave. I was with him the day a wolf got into the chicken coop."

Sitti's hands were gnarled and slow. Amani let them set the pace. The shrak browned on one side before Amani picked it up by the edges to flip it.

"What a commotion! Hens trying to escape. One dead at the wolf's feet. I was sure he'd attack but he stood there, staring at your grandfather. He had eyes of amber. Your grandfather told him to leave and never come back. The wolf growled but picked up the hen in his mouth and fled. Seedo's brothers were all set to hunt him down, but Seedo stopped them. 'He won't bother us again,' he said. And he didn't."

With a piece of warm shrak in one pocket and an orange in the other, Amani walked through her aunt's rose garden. Had Seedo really told off a wolf? No. Sitti was making it up. Yet the story inspired her. No wolf would keep her off Seedo's Peak.

Wire and scraps of tin extended from two fig trees over to the olive grove, fencing in the sheep. Sahem lay sprawled in the morning sun near another fig tree. He wasn't much bigger than a spring lamb but the sheep obeyed him as if he were twice their size. His brown ears perked up at Amani's approach.

"Seedo's Peak!" she said, opening the gate.

Nasty charged out first, followed by the ewes and four lambs, trying to keep up. Sahem herded them into the olive grove.

Amani stopped Black Face and rubbed behind her ears.

"Remember that wolf, and keep your new lamb close. I've named her Survivor."

On the oasis they stopped for a long drink before the hot climb up the slope. The sheep reached the summit and began to graze.

Amani walked slowly back and forth across the peak, searching the dry, flat ground. Nothing. She checked the sheep regularly. Ten.

When she reached the north edge she stopped, alarmed. The yellow bulldozer in the north valley was hard at work. Several cars were parked along the shoulder. It looked like the beginning of a new exit.

What for? A gas station? A store? A checkpoint?

The sight paralyzed her. Her mouth turned dry. They were on her side of the highway. Why not the other side?

Uneasy, she forced herself to turn away and continued her search, ending at the gully.

The placenta was gone.

Amani found what she'd been looking for between some rocks. Wolf scat, remarkably small. His body had made a thorough use of an animal he'd digested, expelling only bits of bone and fur.

Amani scanned every rock in the gully, every crevice and shadow up and around the Camel's Hump, daring the wolf to appear.

She waited a long time. Nothing moved.

ELEVEN

LATE ONE AFTERNOON IN AUGUST, Sahem barked, racing across Seedo's Peak toward the south-east corner. Someone was coming up the path.

Omar.

Amani waved, staying where she sat near the north slope. Was he fed up with the Israeli machines in their vineyards? Or bringing good news? He'd been waiting for the results of the Tawjihi, jumping every time Baba's phone rang.

It was hard to wait for the thing you wanted most in life.

"I thought you might need some intelligent conversation," he said.

"I have the sheep for that. Food would be nice."

He dug in his pocket and offered her a handful of figs. "How did I know."

"Are they past our house?"

He nodded, avoiding her eyes.

The bulldozers had been digging through their fields. Amani was glad to get away from the noises, the cracking vines, the falling canopies, the shovels dumping the heart of their vineyards into a truck.

"Did you watch?"

Omar popped a fig in his mouth. Amani knew from his twisted face that he had, hating the Israeli soldiers and the workmen and how they did what they wanted. Omar hated being powerless to stop them. Amani understood.

"I read that book you gave me," she said. Omar had given her a history book about Al Nakba, the catastrophe. Six hundred thousand Palestinians had evacuated their homes during the war of 1948. Instead of returning in a few weeks, they had become refugees.

He smacked his palm against his forehead. "I forgot to return it. If you go to school, give it back to Miss Aboushi for me."

"Why would I go to school?"

"So you don't sound like Baba when you speak English. You'd love Miss Aboushi. She's teaching your grade next year — "

His eyes widened in alarm. He stared over her shoulder. She turned to see what was wrong.

Two yellow Caterpillars were parked at the foot of the north slope leading up to Seedo's Peak. They'd stopped work for the day. They'd leveled a wide path from the highway to the base of Seedo's mountain.

Omar's eyes narrowed, accusing her.

"When did that start?"

"A month ago. Maybe two. They didn't work all July."

"Why didn't you say anything?"

The tone of his voice dug into her, angry.

"I thought they were building a gas station…"

Spoken out loud, her excuse sounded lame.

Omar hurled a rock down the slope. "They're building a new road. They're coming *here*."

At supper the mood on the porch was gloomy. Ammo Hani muttered the prayer and they ate. Below the porch a long stretch of scraped land ran through the vineyards like an open wound.

Omar chose his words carefully.

"I was on the peak today with Amani. We saw bulldozers at the bottom of the north slope. It looks like they intend to build a road up the north side."

"A road to Seedo's Peak…on the north side?" her uncle repeated.

Amani felt sick. Would he ask the same question Omar had?

He didn't. He had bigger worries.

"What do they want? Do they intend to connect the two valleys?"

"Not over Seedo's Peak," Baba answered quickly. "The grade on the south side above the oasis is too steep."

Ammo Hani nodded. "Unless they're heading for our water."

Amma Fatima shook her head. "How would they know about the spring?"

"Surveillance. Satellites. They've mapped out every part of our lives," Omar said.

Supper cooled in the bowls between them. Sitti urged them to eat. They'd butchered a hen that morning and Amma Fatima had stewed it with lentils and onions. Amani watched Ammo Hani begin to eat. He was too quiet.

Suddenly he stared from Baba to Omar.

"I say we go out tonight and destroy a bulldozer."

Amani struggled to swallow.

"What with?" Baba asked. "Explosives?"

"For once, you have a good idea." Ammo Hani's right hand came down — smack — into his left palm.

Amani stared at Omar. He kept eating, his face expressionless. Opposite him, Mama watched, tense and frowning. She was either going to interrupt or walk home.

"Violence is not the answer," Baba said.

"Tell that to the Israelis. They started it. They punish us. We punish them."

"Think about it, Hani. They have billions of American dollars behind them. You blow up one bulldozer tonight, they'll bring ten more tomorrow. Worse, they'll bring soldiers and tanks. Their Mossad will knock at our door, shoot us or throw us in prison, demolish our houses and the village, too. How does that help anyone?"

No one ate. Amani knew it was true. She'd seen it many times on the news.

Pleading, Baba said, "If you'd only read that book about Ghandi —"

"This is Palestine! Not India!" Ammo Hani roared. "They don't need us digging their ditches or building their swimming pools for a few lousy shekels. Those days are gone. They want our land. Our water. They want to drive us out, village by village. A man has the right to defend himself on his own land."

Amani didn't like the thought of blowing up bulldozers. But listening to her uncle, she agreed. They had a right to defend their homes. She wanted to defend Seedo's Peak.

If only Seedo were here. What would he say?

Baba's phone rang. The opening bars of Mozart's *Eine Kleine Nachtmusik* repeated several times before Baba found and pulled the small silver phone from his shirt pocket. He stared at the screen, pressed a button and held it to his ear.

"Hello," Baba said loudly in English.

Wardeh and her mother began to clear the food no one could finish.

A long pause. "Yes, Miss Aboushi."

Omar's eyes lit up.

"He's sitting right here." Baba loved speaking English with Miss Aboushi.

"No. He's not eating. He looks very thin. I'll tell him." Another pause.

"Thank you. He'll call you later when he decides what to do."

Baba pressed a button and returned the phone to his pocket. He tore off a piece of bread and dipped it into the last bit of stewed chicken.

"Why can't that woman speak Arabic?" Ammo Hani complained.

Amani tried not to smile. She'd understood perfectly when Ammo Hani had not.

"She knows I like to practice my English."

"What did the American say?"

"Why call her the American?" Omar said. "She grew up there, that's all. You criticize those who leave as cowards. She came back with her parents so that makes her the opposite. Baba, what did she say?"

Baba dipped into the bowl of stewed zucchini from Mama's garden. He was the only one eating.

"Eat," Baba mumbled. "It might be your last home-cooked meal for a long time. They want you in Ramallah next week. You've won a scholarship to Birzeit University."

Omar leapt to his feet, whooping with joy. Amani's heart leapt with him. His dream had come true.

"Why is he dancing like that?" Sitti asked. "Is he getting married?"

They began to clap. Omar danced a circle around them, laughing and spinning until he returned to his place and hugged Mama.

Ammo Hani's hands lay silent in his lap. "I haven't said he can go."

Baba's mouth dropped open.

"He doesn't need to go to Birzeit University. Ramallah is full of modern thinking. The girls don't cover their arms or heads. Seedo would never have wanted him to go to Ramallah. He'll never be a devout Muslim there."

Amani nearly shouted. Tyrant! Occupying all of them with his rules.

Baba exploded before Amani did.

"What's wrong with you? If our father were alive, he'd be happy for Omar. It's enough the Israelis steal our land and our water. Why let them steal our children's dreams?"

Ammo Hani's face was four sharp corners. "All these years we've been lucky, but the occupation threatens our valley now. He should stay home. He could study just as easily at the university in Al Khalil."

Baba stared into the valley, hidden now by dusk. His hunched shoulders reminded Amani of Seedo.

"I know you feel responsible for protecting our land. If we're going to survive we have to adapt to change. Remember when we built the first greenhouse for tomatoes? Everyone in the village laughed. Now everyone has a greenhouse. New ideas help us survive. The next generation may find a new solution. Let him go and find it, Hani."

Ammo Hani's breath came out hard, like a horse straining under a heavy load. "We need him here."

"Maybe he'll come back."

Ammo Hani's eyes were shiny. "He's the only son between us."

Ammo Hani's love for Omar pooled in his eyes. It caught Amani off guard. She'd never seen it before.

With a blink the old hard look returned, making her wonder if she'd imagined it.

"Go, if you wish, as long as you're back for the olive harvest. If I learn you're drinking alcohol or going out with girls or not fasting during Ramadan, we'll bring you home tied to the donkey."

Baba's phone rang again.

Amani helped her aunt and Wardeh clear dishes, puzzled that Ammo Hani had listened to Baba. Maybe he did have a heart, even if it was harder and smaller than an uncooked chickpea.

In the kitchen Amma Fatima stirred down a pot of

Turkish coffee. Watching her aunt at her evening ritual made Amani feel safe. Chubby and strong, Amma Fatima could scrub her house, Sitti's and a sick neighbor's all before breakfast. She cooked enormous meals and was devoted to her family, visitors with gossip, and her rose garden. She never read or listened to Mama play the piano, yet Mama loved her and relied on her. Amani suddenly realized that she did, too.

When Amani took the coffee tray to the porch, Mama held the phone and was wiping tears from her cheek.

"Goodbye. Tell her I'm coming," she said, giving Baba back the phone.

Mama never cried. Who was she talking to? Where was she going?

They were quiet while Mama composed herself.

"My mother's dying of cancer. The doctors give her a month or two to get her affairs in order. She wants to see me before she dies. My brothers can buy a ticket from Amman to Toronto. I'd fly out of Jordan if I could get there."

Mama rarely talked about the past. Amani knew only a few facts about her other grandmother. As a young girl she'd witnessed the massacre of her village in 1948 when the Jewish defence forces had attacked. Orphaned, she was raised in Jerusalem, then married a man from a village near Bethlehem. Amani nicknamed her Musical Sitti because she'd taught Mama to play the piano. When that village was confiscated by Israel, she'd taken her sons to Canada. Only Mama remained, inheriting the piano and a fear of living in a village.

Ammo Hani shook his head. "Why would you risk traveling with all the roadblocks and checkpoints?"

"I have to see her." Mama's face was unhappy. "But I don't want my brothers to buy my ticket. I'd rather sell my piano than let them think we can't buy our own." She lifted her chin proudly.

How could Mama sell her piano? What was happening to the adults tonight?

Baba squeezed Mama's hand. "Not your piano. Your mother gave it to you. I can sell my books —"

Mama yanked her hand away. They were heading for a fight.

Ammo Hani's voice was firm. "For once tonight we will respect our traditions. I've made a decision and it's final."

He paused to sip his coffee, enjoying the moment.

"Let your brothers pay for your ticket. It's your mother's wish. There's nothing more important," he nodded at Sitti, "than making a mother happy. There will be no more discussions about coming and going. Omar goes to Ramallah. Rose goes to Canada. And that piano! The piano stays in the valley."

TWELVE

AMANI CURLED UP ON the dark green sofa. Her mother's fingers flew over the keyboard. No music sat on the wooden ledge.

Amani thought of Sitti. Her hands made bread though her brain forgot the recipe. Maybe memory lived in every part of the body, in limbs that had practiced something daily over many years, not just in brain cells.

Mama leaned into the piano. Amani let her mind snap a photo and memorize the image, a dyed streak of blonde hair curled over Mama's forehead, the lines in her face almost smooth.

The music stopped, lingering into a few beats of silence.

It was hard to imagine Mama not here.

Amani began to cry.

She felt her mother's arms around her.

"I didn't know you liked Chopin so much."

Amani looked into her mother's brown eyes. She was teasing.

"I wish you weren't going tomorrow."

"If you were in my shoes, would you visit me before I died?"

"Of course!"

"I wish you'd met her. You'd love your grandmother. I was only a few years older than you when we had to leave our village and live in a camp. When they decided to move to Canada, I cried for weeks. My mother understood how my love of Palestine was like my lungs."

"Take lots of videos. Make her tell stories, Mama. About how she became a Christian. And about you. You never talk about the past. I want to know everything!"

"Really?"

"Really."

Mama looked out the window.

"The past has a way of ruining the present, but maybe it's time you knew more." She turned to face Amani. "When your father and I married, Hani was the one who made Seedo accept the infidel into the family."

Amani's mouth went dry. She shook her head in disbelief. "Seedo?" she whispered. "Seedo didn't accept you?"

"He refused to attend our wedding. He wouldn't let Sitti come. Sitti cried for weeks. Then she got mad and moved in with Fatima."

"Did...did Seedo apologize?"

"No! They didn't speak to each other for months. Hani was desperate. So he came to Jerusalem with Sitti and

Fatima. Hani begged your father and me to come and live in the valley. He offered to share his inheritance. Hani was the one who brokered peace, of a kind, for the family."

Amani's head was spinning. "And then? Seedo accepted you then, didn't he?"

Mama rolled her eyes. "He was a very stubborn man, your grandfather. That's why we live over here on the other side of the valley."

"Because of Seedo?"

Mama nodded. "Then I got pregnant. It's amazing what a baby can do to a family. Sitti began to invite us to her porch for supper. If Seedo wanted to eat, he had to eat with us. We spent nine months arguing about religion until Sitti threatened to move back to Al Khalil. We reached a compromise. I agreed Seedo could teach my children to love Allah."

"Was that hard?"

"God, Jehovah, Allah—the name was no longer important to me. I wanted peace. My brothers tell me that in Canada the native people call it the Great Spirit. I like that."

"Why didn't anyone ever tell me?"

"Why bring up an unhappy time? Remember how your grandfather would say that when he surrendered to Allah, there was no anger in his heart? He became thankful both sons lived in the valley. Your grandfather was a devout and wonderful man." Mama laughed, shaking her fist like Ammo Hani. "As long as we used the word Allah."

The sound of Omar and Baba at the kitchen door made Mama turn and call, "What did you find out?"

The conversation detoured to travel plans. For a few minutes Amani tried to listen. Baba spread out a map. Mama and Omar would go to Kalandia, the checkpoint hub between Jerusalem and Ramallah. From there Mama would take a taxi to the border and cross the Allenby Bridge. Omar would carry on to Ramallah.

Checkpoints, long lineups — Amani couldn't listen. The room crowded in around her. She longed to be under the open sky on Seedo's Peak where she could think about her grandfather. No one noticed her leave.

Outside she called Sahem to bring the sheep. They were grazing the sparse slope above her house with a neighbor's goats.

Amani hated crossing back over the scraped, bare ground where the vineyards had once grown. Up and down the valley everyone talked about how to stop the Israelis from the next step: paving it. Amani ran until she was in the olive grove. Then her mind returned to Mama's story, and Seedo.

Her grandfather had been a tyrant. It made her mind flip upside-down and sideways. Slowly her thoughts began to settle, slightly rearranged. Even though he'd been so hard on her parents, her love for him hadn't changed. It was as if her mind had kept a black-and-white photo of Seedo, and now the image had color.

Her feet moved automatically. She reached the top of the path, surprised to realize she stood on the peak. Above her the sky was a dazzling white. Near the gully she found a comfortable spot facing east and leaned against a rock, her back to the sun.

It was hot. She closed her eyes.

What was that? She scrambled to her feet, one hand on her chest. Her skin felt cool. Quickly she counted the sheep, still grazing, but near the path home. Ten.

She whirled around to stare into the gully, knowing what she'd see before her eyes found him.

The wolf stood as if he'd just emerged from the rock beneath his paws. He was smaller than she remembered, and so close she could see the color of his eyes. Yellow.

His ears and tail were up. He was watching her intently, waiting. What for?

Just like the last time, her body itched to run away.

She waved her crook and yelled, "Go away!"

He disappeared between the boulders. The last thing Amani saw was the pale tip of his tail.

Amani stared after him in shock. She'd scared him away.

Then she noticed something that made her forget the wolf.

There were small X's painted on a line of rocks in the gully. Her heart tumbled over a sheer cliff. She couldn't breathe.

How long had the X's been there? A few hours? Days?

The Israelis were going to build a settlement on Seedo's Peak.

THIRTEEN

WITHOUT MAMA AND OMAR the house had empty spaces. In the same way her tongue searched for a tooth after it was gone, every time Amani passed the piano or Baba's desk where her brother used to study, her eyes lingered, missing them.

After supper she laid out six mattresses on Seedo's porch. Baba stood on the steps, staring across the valley at their dark house.

"I'm sorry. I'd rather sleep at home."

Amma Fatima told him not to apologize.

"I'll go with you, Baba," Amani said. She couldn't delay sharing the bad news any longer.

Baba's steps faltered as she told him about the X's. He groaned, saying nothing until he opened the side door into the unlit hallway. The piano keys reflected a ghostly bit of light.

"They'll put up a fence soon." His voice was flat.

Amani wished Mama were here to say the right thing. All Amani could do was turn on a light.

"Did you see any settlers? Soldiers? Anyone on the peak?"

"No."

He mulled this over. "Where will you take the sheep if you can't graze there?"

Without Seedo's Peak, she'd have to share the overgrazed south slope with their neighbor's flocks.

"I'll find somewhere."

Baba put a finger to his lips, reminding her of Seedo. "I'll tell Hani, but not tonight. It will only ruin his sleep. I want to make some phone calls first. I'm organizing a protest against the highway."

Baba must have told Ammo Hani the bad news the next day. Without a word, he began to disappear on the donkey every evening before coffee.

Once, sometimes twice a week, Mama or Omar phoned with news. In Canada Musical Sitti planned to live forever now that Mama was at her side. Amani forced a laugh, trying to sound happy. Omar loved Birzeit and meeting other students. He'd joined a political group. They were planning a protest. It sounded safer than the valley.

She didn't tell him about the X's. Neither did Baba.

Every morning Amani ordered Sahem to keep the sheep on the oasis while she climbed the steep path alone. With each step, her stomach rose a little higher until it crouched in her throat, until the view opened and she could see across the mountaintop. When she knew they were alone, she swallowed her fear for another day and called Sahem.

Each day she could still graze the sheep on Seedo's Peak felt like a blessing. When she heard the call to prayer, she prayed the words Seedo had taught her, *Allahu Akbar*.

The yellow machines made steady progress up the north slope of Seedo's Peak while on the south side, in their narrow valley, it stayed strangely quiet. The construction workers stared at Amani when she watched them from the north edge, then ignored her. She imagined what they saw. A Palestinian girl alone with a few sheep. Hardly a threat.

As the machines approached the summit, Amani felt as if she were trapped in an hourglass. Time began to accelerate, funnelling down, grains pouring faster. The last day of August became her last hours on her grandfather's land, then the slippery rush as hours became minutes. The workers were so close Amani could smell their coffee.

Late in the afternoon several trucks drove onto the peak and parked. Men swarmed around the back and began to unload long metal poles and coils of barbed wire. A soldier with a gun stood beside them and made a motion for Amani to move away.

Amani wanted to yell at them. This had been her ancestors' land for more than a thousand years. A construction worker stopped to share a joke with the soldier. They both laughed, giving her a strange look.

Then she was afraid. She was alone, far from the valley. They were men. They had guns.

She gave a hand signal to Sahem and walked away, driving the sheep toward the south-east corner and the path home.

Safety came first. But she hated walking away and feeling like a coward.

On the Camel's Hump a wink of light caught her eye. She stared at the spot. Everything facing the setting sun was turning rosy-pink.

Was it a reflection off a wolf's eyes?

She scanned the hump. Nothing moved.

Black Face moved toward the gully to graze, her lamb close. Behind Amani, Sahem barked near the path. Were they going home?

Not yet.

She climbed on a rock and stared across the peak. The men were climbing into the truck. She shouted, "*Rouh!* Go away!"

The truck started up and disappeared over the northern edge. Amani shook her fist at them and was about to shout again when she heard a fierce bark that made her turn.

Across the gully, the wolf stood on a rock, looking up at the Camel's Hump. His tail was straight out and his lips were curled, displaying his teeth. His front legs lowered, the bend in his limbs so quick that Amani's knees gave out.

Amani shouted at Black Face, "Run!"

From the other side of the gully, above the wolf, a terrible sound answered her. The crack of a rifle shot. The wolf crouched low to the ground. A ping of rock dust rose by his front paw. Then he was gone between the big boulders.

A second crack.

Black Face fell to the ground. Dark red blood spurted from her head, oozing onto her back. Shocked, Amani jumped off the rock, then stared up at the Camel's Hump.

A man with a beard and circle hat stood where Amani had seen the wink of light a few minutes earlier. Beside him stood a boy Omar's age. Long brown curls grew wild around his face. From his neck hung a pair of black binoculars.

Settlers.

The boy shouted something in English that sounded like, "No! Dad…" followed by a string of unintelligible words.

The man lifted his rifle again. The boy reached up —

Amani didn't wait. She grabbed Survivor, screaming at Sahem to take the sheep home. He was already barking, driving them off the peak. Amani ran to the path, fearing a third and final crack. She leapt over rocks, zigzagging to safety.

Partway down the slope, she released Survivor, too big to carry. They scrambled after the others. How long would it take a man to cross the gully? Then she remembered his rifle. The only place to hide was the olive grove. The trees had never seemed so far.

Terrified, Amani ran across the open oasis, Survivor beside her.

The instant she was among the olive trees, she ducked behind a tree and looked back. No one followed. She held a hand on her chest to quiet her heart, still racing. Branches, limbs and leaves rose in a protective shield around her.

The grove lay in shadow. There were no sounds of pursuit, only the suck of her breath as it returned to normal, and the bleating of the sheep waiting to be let into the pen.

FOURTEEN

AMMA FATIMA AND WARDEH were arranging the last plates of supper on the porch. Since Mama's departure Amma Fatima fussed over Amani. When Amani sat beside her father, her aunt observed her closely.

"What's wrong? Something happened. Tell us."

With a heavy heart, Amani told them how the Israeli trucks had arrived on the peak and unloaded fencing material. She took a breath.

"Black Face got shot by a settler."

Ammo Hani leapt to his feet, exploding like a bomb. "Didn't I tell you what would happen? Settlers!"

Baba tried to calm him. "You know we couldn't have stopped them. You know they'll claim the peak is uninhabited land. We'll take it to court. They're breaking international laws."

"Whose courts? Their courts! We'll waste our money and time. We'll join the long list of Palestinian land claims. No! We fight them now while we have a chance."

"How, Hani? They're better armed."

"In the Qur'an we're taught to fight against those who

would destroy us. We have resistance fighters. A sniper, well positioned — "

"If you kill a settler, the violence will escalate," Baba interrupted. Cigarette smoke curled from his mouth, a new habit since Mama's departure. "Be patient, Hani. I have friends helping me organize a protest."

"Protests." Ammo Hani spat out the word. "The Israelis laugh at our protests. Tomorrow they pave the highway. Then they'll take the rest of our land. A man has the right to defend his land. I can at least blow up the fence."

Baba's voice rose. "What will that do? They'll rebuild. But first they'll punish all of us, everyone in the village, too."

Ammo Hani paced like a caged animal. Suddenly he stopped and pointed at Amani.

"No more shepherd for you, girl."

Amani panicked. She was about to lose her sheep.

"I have Sahem with me and — "

"What protection is a dog? They'll shoot the dog, then the sheep, then you. There won't be a witness, as if that mattered. We'll go up and find your dead body."

Baba nodded grimly. "He's right, Amani. It's not worth the risk."

"Why are you taking his side?" Amani cried out. "I'm old enough — "

"You're old enough for a soldier to do what he wants with you if he finds you alone," Ammo Hani shouted.

It was growing darker with every angry word. Amma Fatima rose and lit a lantern. The smell of kerosene killed Amani's appetite. She folded her arms across her chest.

Ammo Hani's jaw was rigid. "We need a new truck. New irrigation pipes. We're going to sell the sheep."

How could she save them? Amani heard Seedo's voice in her head, guiding her through a confrontation. *Respect his dignity.*

Ammo Hani felt responsible. He worried for her safety.

Amani took a deep breath and unfolded her arms.

"You're right, Ammo Hani. I promise you I will never take them on the peak again. Never. You were right. It's not safe up there."

It was an easy promise to make. There would be a fence around the peak in a few days.

"I will only graze them where it's safe. Along the valley or above my house. Never on Seedo's Peak, I promise."

Ammo Hani hitched up his pants. "Fine. Tend the sheep a while longer. Their days are numbered with ours unless we fight back."

He stormed off the porch without eating. The donkey brayed. Then they heard hoofs clopping on the road into the village. Amma Fatima sighed and went into the kitchen to make coffee.

FIFTEEN

AMANI WOKE TO THE SOUND of Baba's phone ringing.

She dressed quickly and left the house with her father, walking across the valley toward Seedo's house. The muezzin began the first call to prayer. Amani stared up at Seedo's Peak. It felt as if someone had lowered a cage over the valley.

"We're protesting today."

For the first time in weeks Amani heard excitement in her father's voice.

"What?" she asked, wondering what there was to be excited about. The damage was done. Thirty meters had been cleared from the heart of everyone's fields. Narrow strips of vineyard on either side would not fill their truck with fruit at harvest time.

"What are you protesting?"

Baba was too engrossed in his plans to catch her tone.

"They're starting to pave today."

Amani remembered the phone call, waking her. "Did you get a permit?"

Baba laughed. "Something better. A reporter. My

friends are bringing a journalist with a camera. They'll be here in two hours for our protest. I'm going to hitch the wagon to the tractor. Don't go far."

In the pen, Amani fed Survivor some of the ewes' milk from a bottle, holding the warm woolly body in her arms. The other sheep waited at the gate, hungry, thirsty. She took them up through the olive grove and filled the trough with water. She leaned on her shepherd's crook, keeping her back to Seedo's mountain.

Sahem waited, ears perked, but she gave no signal. Where could she take the sheep to graze? She looked up and down the valley, then at the south slope above her house. Other neighbors took their goats and sheep there. It was all overgrazed.

Without access to clean pastureland she had nowhere to graze her small flock.

She walked slowly beside the low stone wall, staring up at the rocky slope.

Seedo's voice spoke inside her. *It's there.*

The path. The one that led to the Firdoos.

Where? She saw nothing but boulders on the slope above the wall. Discouraged, she let the sheep graze in the upper olive terraces until she heard the tractor start up.

The family sat in the wagon, waiting for her. Wardeh moved over to make room. The wagon bounced onto the road. Everyone careened into each other and laughed. Except Amani.

She didn't smile until her uncle amazed her by starting a chant. "No more highways! This is our land!"

Wardeh clapped and chanted with her father. Amma Fatima lifted a hand over her mouth and ululated, a high trilling sound from the back of her throat.

When Sitti began to clap and chant, Amani finally laughed. She had to join in.

"Nabil! Join us! Yassar!" Baba called to two men working in the fields.

One by one, men left the fields to fall in behind them. As they approached the village, people left the old stone houses, small gardens, even the mosque to join them. Baba turned left and led a long procession down the tractor path toward the new highway.

Amani twisted to see the paved section of the settlers' highway that curved west toward Al Khalil. Trucks, rollers and workmen in hardhats were laying asphalt over the new section.

Two cars with yellow license plates were parked nearby on the shoulder. Three men and a woman waved at Baba. One held a big camera, filming. Two wore red baseball caps. The third man made Amani nervous. He wore a circle hat like the settlers.

Baba waved and shouted at them, "*Salam! Shalom!* Come! Join us!"

He drove out of the vineyard and onto the gravel, ahead of the area being paved.

The procession became a human blockade across the highway. Baba shut off the engine and jumped down. The man and woman wearing baseball caps had joined the men and boys wearing farm gloves, the women wearing hijab, the crying babies and the toddlers clutching their mothers' long skirts. Last in line was an elderly man in a wheelbarrow pushed by a teenager.

The man with the camera took pictures of everybody.

The man with the circle hat strode toward Baba and gave him a hug. Nothing shocked Amani more than seeing her father hug that man.

Smiling, Baba introduced the rabbi to the family in the wagon. Stunned, all Amani could manage was a slight nod. Her uncle's face was guarded and unfriendly.

Sitti, however, stood and held out her hand to shake the rabbi's.

"*Ahlan.* When I was a little girl in Al Khalil, a rabbi lived in the Jews Quarter beside us," she said warmly. "He was a very nice man."

Amani stared in amazement at her father. Baba had organized this. Baba knew a rabbi. Baba had friends who came to help when he phoned them.

In the distance dark green army jeeps sped down the highway toward them. The protesters chanted and clapped. Construction work halted and the men in hard hats gathered behind soldiers.

Loaded with soldiers, the jeeps parked between the Palestinians and the construction workers. Dozens of rifles pointed at the human blockade as one jeep pulled close to the wagon. Dust rose from the dirt. When it settled, a soldier left the jeep and approached Baba.

Amani's pride turned to fear. Her father was the obvious leader. On the news she'd seen Palestinian leaders dragged off to prison.

The soldier was a small man with a big voice. Amani guessed he was the commanding officer. He spoke fluent Arabic.

"Where's your permit to hold a protest?" he said, poking Baba's chest.

"Where's your permit to build a highway and settlement on Arab land? We haven't given our permission for any of this."

Half her father's age, the officer had an air of someone who didn't expect to be questioned. He pointed at the reporter and shouted in English, "No pictures! No camera!"

Then the officer stared at the family in the wagon behind Baba. When his gaze flicked over her, Amani shivered. But it settled on Sitti.

He switched to Arabic. "If you don't leave this highway

immediately, I'll put you all in prison. Is that your mother? I've seen your women cheer after their sons blow up innocent people. What kind of mother does that? I have no sympathy for your mothers. We'll start with her."

A flame of anger ignited inside Amani. How dare he insult Sitti?

Amani turned to Sitti. "Are you afraid?"

Sitti shook her head. "I'm an old woman. I've said my prayers all my life. I'm not afraid of him."

"Let's stand beside Baba."

Amani helped her grandmother climb out the back of the wagon. Sitti was shorter than the officer. She looked up and wagged a finger at him as if he were a naughty child.

"Be careful how you talk to my son," Sitti said.

Amani guessed Sitti had forgotten their names. It didn't matter.

"And my granddaughter. And my village. Take me to prison. You're making me very tired so you'll have to take me sitting down."

Sitti sank to the ground. Amani stared at the commander.

Before she lost her courage, Amani said, "Me, too," and sat beside Sitti.

Immediately Ammo Hani, Amma Fatima and Wardeh left the wagon and joined them cross-legged on the ground. Without a word, all the villagers sat, including the two strangers in red baseball caps.

Baba was the last to sit, nearly on the boots of the commander.

Only the rabbi remained standing. He spoke in Hebrew to the officer, gesturing frequently at the passive, seated protest. The anger gradually left the officer's eyes, but his face remained stony.

Then the rabbi sat beside Baba.

The photographer was quietly taking pictures. Either the officer ignored him or he was too busy giving orders to notice. Construction workers and soldiers headed for their vehicles.

"Sit." The officer shrugged. "Sit all day if you like. Any Palestinian interfering with construction tomorrow will be shot. This is a security zone."

When the last jeep left, the protesters stood and cheered. Amma Fatima began to ululate. Amani and Wardeh joined her, all the other women, too. It felt wonderful to cheer together. Then they hugged one other, laughing with relief. The line broke into small groups, discussing what they might do next. Baba and the rabbi moved among the groups, talking to everyone. People began to leave. It was time to go back to their chores.

Amani hated to see the groups break away. She stayed beside Wardeh and Wardeh's cousin on her mother's side,

Raja'. They begged Baba and the rabbi to translate everything the officer had said.

"He's following orders. He has to protect the highway."

Ammo Hani shook his fist. "If he'd poked me, I'd have broken his jaw."

"Never touch a soldier!" Baba said, and the rabbi agreed.

Amani shook hands with the peacemakers in the red baseball caps. She shook hands with the reporter. In spite of how strange it felt, she shook hands with the rabbi. He smiled at her. His eyes were pale blue.

Squished beside Wardeh and Raja' in the back of the wagon, Amani joined the merriment, teasing the slow-pokes they passed on the village road until, in the distance, she saw a chain-link fence partially erected around Seedo's Peak. Topped by a coil of barbed wire, it resembled a crown of thorns.

"That was a lovely wedding!" Sitti exclaimed.

Everyone laughed so hard they began to cry, and Amani looked away, crying, too.

After supper Baba suggested they sleep over with Fatima's family on Seedo's porch. There were no arguments. Ammo Hani didn't disappear on the donkey. Baba phoned Omar, then Mama, and told them about the protest.

In the dark, Amani half-listened to Baba. Settlers were

coming to live behind that fence on Seedo's Peak. What would they be like? Were they all going to be like the one who'd shot Black Face?

She thought about the settler's son. She wished she'd understood what he'd yelled. He'd wanted to stop his father. If her new neighbors spoke English and she had to protect her sheep from them, she needed to understand them.

Baba brought her the phone. It was wonderful to hear Mama's voice.

"I've made a decision, Mama," Amani said.

"What's that?"

"I want to study English with Miss Aboushi."

Across an ocean, on waves of sound, Amani heard Mama's mouth drop open.

"I'm going to school."

SIXTEEN

UP THROUGH THE OLIVE TERRACES, Amani herded
the sheep slowly, letting them nibble anything they could
find. Summer dust stirred under their feet.

Amani walked beside the wall below the Camel's
Hump. Seedo had said the Firdoos were beyond the hump.
Her ancestors had cleared rocks from the small plateau and
chiseled them with care to build the long retaining wall.
Had they built the wall to hide a path?

The sheep gathered around the trough, bleating with
impatience. Amani filled it and returned to walk beside the
wall, her gaze on the slope of boulders. She'd passed it a
thousand times, scanned it from every possible angle.
What had she missed?

Aware of a fresh, large sheep patty on the ground in
front of her, Amani shifted her gaze to avoid it. She wore
her old pair of shoes and rarely cared where she stepped.
Pats of sheep dung littered the ground in various dried-out
sizes.

Two steps ahead something unusual caught her attention. She knelt to examine the short, round bit of scat.

Mostly hair and bone. Except it was white, maybe a week old.

The wolf had been on the oasis.

She stared at the wall directly in front of the scat. Every rock had settled into place a long time ago, held by mortar and, if she remembered Omar's physics, pressure.

She laid her crook on top of the wall and climbed up to crouch on the rough flat surface. Survivor bleated, too small to make the leap. Amani reached down and hoisted her up.

"Silly lamb. But since you're here, maybe you could find me a path."

Amani stood, leaning into the slope. Hands and feet splayed frog-like over the boulders and she began to climb, searching.

Beside her, then ahead, Survivor bounded up several boulders and disappeared.

"Survivor?"

Out of sight, Survivor bleated from farther up the slope.

Amani crawled to where she thought Survivor had disappeared. She peered over the boulder under her hands. There was a space between the boulders — a space wide enough for an animal.

A path.

Invisible from below, a narrow path ghosted up toward

the south side of the Camel's Hump. At the first curve she lost sight of it and Survivor.

Amani's heart raced. "Wait, Survivor! We're coming!"

Excited, she scrambled back to the top of the wall for her crook. She ordered Sahem to bring the sheep.

"Yalla!" she cried.

One after the other, the sheep leapt onto the wall, up a few boulders and disappeared. Sahem followed, Amani last.

Beside her the boulders were almost waist high. It was hard to believe the path was real. She glanced back, reassured to see the top of the stone wall in both directions. Below it, the oasis looked the same, water trough at one end, olive terraces at the other.

The climb was narrow and steep. It headed constantly east, wrapping up and around the south side of the hump. She could see the route of the Israeli highway as the valley veered south. Behind her she couldn't see the oasis anymore.

Ahead the path began to widen. Amani couldn't see the flock but she heard them, and Sahem, on the twisting path above.

How long had she been climbing? Half an hour, maybe longer. She kept her feet moving until at last the grade became more gradual, and then she was out of the boulders. The tip of the Camel's Hump was behind her, blocking a view of Seedo's Peak.

There was no path ahead on the flat ground. Her sheep grazed peacefully.

Amani relaxed. She rewarded Sahem with a quick pat. "Good dog."

Dusty, desolate peaks rode the horizon around a long plateau in front of them. It felt like a hidden world.

In the east the sun blazed in an early morning sky the way it had in the valley. The land was dry but offered more scrubby vegetation than the valley. Amani gripped Seedo's crook. Under her fingers the wood felt reassuringly familiar.

"What do you say, Sahem? Which way?"

Tail wagging, he barked.

"East. Just what I was thinking," Amani said, herding the sheep toward the rugged peak at the end of the plateau.

A spot of green along the north-facing edge turned out to be a wide crevice protected from the sun. Amani sat in its shade while her sheep found more to eat in an hour than they had all week.

The morning passed at a relaxed pace, the way it used to with Seedo. When they finally reached the base of the far craggy slope, she let the animals fan out to graze. Part way up, an enormous pile of boulders jutted out from the slope like a long balcony.

Wild carrot grew in the shade of a fissure. They were Mama's favorite summer flower. A bouquet blossomed in

Amani's fist as she explored, poking cautiously around the rocks.

Just before the fissure ended, Amani discovered a natural stairway leading up through the rocks. It headed to one side of the balcony.

Sahem barked at her. Amani ordered him to wait with the sheep.

It was a steep but easy climb. When she reached the last step, Amani gasped.

Behind the balcony was a small mountain meadow, lush and green with grass. Above it, a stream gushed from a spring bringing water to the ground in front of the balcony.

Nothing moved on the rocky hillside above. Amani's eyes swept the meadow twice before they grew wide with fear.

On the far side, a man lay in the long grass, his back to Amani. His dull green T-shirt had camouflaged his shoulders. The unnatural blue of his jeans had snagged Amani's attention. His head was bushy with wild brown hair.

A young man? The settler's son?

He lay flat on the ground, his head and shoulders propped up by his elbows, peering at the rocky slope above the meadow through binoculars.

What he was studying so intently? Were other settlers exploring ahead? How had he found the path to the Firdoos?

Then she remembered how loudly she'd called to Survivor after she'd disappeared on the hidden path. How visible she must have been to anyone observing her from Seedo's Peak.

The boy had followed her. Made his way to the Firdoos — unobserved — while she'd relaxed, grazing her sheep.

The thought sickened her. Amani groaned out loud.

The boy's head twisted sharply. He scrambled to his feet, yelling something in English. Amani dropped the bouquet and fled, praying she wasn't running straight into his father's rifle.

SEVENTEEN

"HURRY UP, AMANI!"

Wardeh's third impatient shout from the driveway found Amani still in the sheep pen. Amani let Survivor suck the last drops of milk from the bottle.

Her historic first day of school was not off to a good start.

Why did Wardeh and Raja' have to leave so early? The sheep crowded behind Amani as she ran to the gate, accusing her of desertion.

"I'll be back this afternoon," Amani said, slipping out and shoving the bolt into place. "Baba's going to let you graze around the fields while he's working. I'll try to take you to the Firdoos again."

Yesterday she'd fled across the plateau to the path descending through the boulders. It ended abruptly just above the long retaining wall. Ahead, the space between the boulders was filled in with small rocks. Amani climbed out of the path onto the boulder below, helped Survivor, and scrambled down to the wall.

They were back. Safe. She'd be more careful next time.

Quiet and quick. She didn't want to run into that boy with the binoculars.

Hurrying up the mountain to school, Wardeh interrupted Amani's thoughts.

"Raja' and I won't wait for you tomorrow if you take so long."

Ever since Amani could remember, Raja' had walked along the village road at dawn to call on Wardeh. Together the two girls had crossed the valley to follow the path above Amani's house.

Amani tried to imagine the Sheep Girl arriving alone at school. How would she endure a whole day in that building?

"The orphan lamb needs a bottle every morning — "

"Don't act like a backward farm girl," Wardeh scolded. "Nobody cares about sheep."

Wardeh set such a fast pace, they had to stop talking until the dirt path leveled off at the summit. They were on a concrete sidewalk in front of small apartments and houses. The big sister pep talk wasn't over.

"Fix your hijab."

"Don't speak to boys privately," Raja' added.

Why had she said she'd go to school? What a stupid idea.

"And tomorrow morning, be careful where you step. You even smell like a sheep."

"Baaa."

"Try to fit in!"

Fit in? She was a shepherd.

As soon as they arrived in the schoolyard, a dozen older girls surrounded Wardeh and Raja', forming a wall that Amani didn't know how to penetrate. She felt like an orphan sheep, listening to snippets of the girls' conversations.

"Is that the Sheep Girl?"

"You got a new iPod!"

"Is your father going to let you apply to university?"

This last question was directed to Wardeh. She glanced furtively at Amani before she whispered her reply.

Amani stared at her cousin's stiff back, puzzled. For all her bossiness, it was hard to imagine Wardeh defying her father. Did she really want to go to university, or was she trying to impress her friends?

The morning classes of math and science dragged by like a hot day without water. There were fourteen girls in her class and they eyed her cautiously. Amani sat at the back, eagerly answering the teachers' questions. Sometimes one of the girls turned around and stared at her. The Sheep Girl hoped she was making a good impression.

At lunch the girls ran outside to eat in a noisy circle. Thirteen backs formed another wall.

"…she's a show-off." Whispers, loud enough for Amani to hear.

Amani's cheeks burned bright red. Yes, she'd impressed them. The wrong way. It was too late to keep quiet. Too late to fit in. Worse, she'd forgotten a lunch. She wouldn't beg from Wardeh.

Amani's stomach growled. Only her hunger to learn English made her stay for the afternoon.

When Miss Aboushi entered the classroom, Amani sat up and stared. Miss Aboushi wore no hijab, her black hair pinned into a modest bun at the back of her head. But as soon as the teacher began to speak, Amani's discomfort returned. She couldn't understand a word the small, energetic woman said, except that no Arabic was to be spoken in English class.

One by one the girls stood in front of the class to talk about what they'd done that summer. Classmates were allowed to ask questions if interested. Amani began to feel more hopeful. She understood them perfectly. They all sounded like Baba, only they giggled and stuttered and used very few verbs.

Miss Aboushi corrected each girl, making her repeat a word or sentence. Amani listened carefully, softly repeating everything her teacher said. It felt like music lessons with Mama.

Then a girl whose small, nervous movements reminded

Amani of a bird stood at the front. "My name Souad. I…go…"

"Went, Souad. Where did you go? Use the past tense."

"I went…nowhere."

All the girls laughed in a friendly way. Souad grinned back.

"I help…help-ed my father."

"The past tense ending sounds like a *t*. Have you forgotten everything over the summer? Repeat after me. Helped." Miss Aboushi spat out an exaggerated *t* of the past tense.

Amani repeated the new word several times

"What kind of help, Souad?"

With small, quick movements her hands made a square in the air. Then she pretended to wrap and place things inside it.

"Ahh. Did you pack things for your father?"

"I peck things for my father."

"Not peck. A bird pecks. Pack." Miss Aboushi said, repeating both verbs slowly as she wrote each on the board. She reminded Amani of Mama when she played almost identical chords on the piano, and made her name them.

"Now say it in the past tense and don't forget the *t*."

"I packed things for my father. Settlers break window. Settlers write bad words on store. No tourists come. He close…closed…store."

Miss Aboushi reached out and squeezed Souad's hand gently.

Amani felt sad for her, but less lonely, too. Souad knew about settlers.

"Thank you, Souad. Yes, you may sit down. I'm letting our new student go last. I thought it would be easier if she had a chance to learn from all of you. I hope you're all being kind to our new student. You know what the Prophet, may his name be praised, said about kindness?"

Miss Aboushi's voice rose, and that was the only way Amani understood that the little speech ended in a question. So many words she didn't understand!

Miss Aboushi was staring at her, as were the other girls. It was her turn to introduce herself. She felt like an animal about to be slaughtered.

Amani shrank into her desk, staring at the black-and-white tiles of the floor.

"Come. Don't be shy. We're very kind."

What did it mean, kind? Amani wished she'd brought her dictionary. She felt stupid. Everyone was watching. Waiting.

Pride forced Amani to her feet, then to the front of the class. She couldn't look at them. Did she smell? Did they think she was a show-off? Would they laugh at her because her accent was so bad?

"Start with your name."

"Amani Raheem," she mumbled.

"Good. You understand English very well, don't you, Amani?"

Amani shook her head, trying to prevent Miss Aboushi's praise in front of the others. Everyone laughed. Unhappy, Amani looked up. All the girls, except the pretty one named Diala, were smiling.

Had she said something funny? Or foolish?

"You do understand English, don't you, Amani?" Miss Aboushi said gently.

"A little." Amani held out a tiny space between her thumb and index finger.

"I taught your brother, Omar. I know you were home-schooled for many years. Can you tell us what brought you to high school?"

Too fast. Amani stared at Miss Aboushi, confused.

Miss Aboushi slowed down. "Why did you come to school today?"

Now Amani couldn't find the English words fast enough. Every verb had gone into hiding. Her eyes lit on a piece of chalk.

Quickly she drew Seedo's Peak and the Camel's Hump on the board.

"My sido…"

"Grandfather," Miss Aboushi corrected. "Only English in this class."

"My grandfather…his mountain. No now…"

All the English words were hiding in a deep brain cave. Amani drew a fence around the lower, flat peak. A man with a circle hat holding a gun.

Miss Aboushi nodded sadly. The girls had similar expressions.

"Settlers." Miss Aboushi gave her the word.

"Settlers," Amani repeated, mimicking perfectly. "Settlers come. Settlers' fence. Settlers take my grandfather's mountain. I love my grandfather's mountain."

She drew a sheep.

"My sheep."

Then she drew a girl. She pointed at the sheep, the girl, then herself. Why had she forgotten the most important English word?

"You are a shepherd," Miss Aboushi said, smiling. "Omar told me."

"Shepherd. Yes." Amani felt her face burning up. She remembered her cousin's warning not to talk about sheep, but how could she not?

"I am shepherd. Settler kill one…my sheep. Settlers speak English. I need English. I need stop them."

No one laughed. There was a hush in the classroom. Souad's eyes were misty. So were Allia's. Dana's. Haniah's, too.

They flooded Amani with questions. What were the

names of her sheep? Did she have a favorite? Did she have time to get ice cream after school? No? When could they meet?

That night, Amani fell asleep happier than she'd felt in a long time. How much she'd learned in a single day. Not only English, but about the other girls, and Wardeh, too.

Amani smiled, imagining her cousin's surprise in the morning when she explained why she was ready so early. She'd agreed to meet her classmates before school. They wanted to hear how Romania came to the valley.

EIGHTEEN

IN SEPTEMBER THE DAYS grew shorter while Amani's sentences in English became longer. Her ability to mimic Miss Aboushi astonished her classmates. Only Diala kept an unfriendly distance. The other girls confided that Diala had been the top student among them. Now Amani occupied that place.

When Omar and Mama phoned, Amani chatted happily about school and her new friends, giving the phone to her father when they asked how things were in the valley.

But walking home from school, she could not avoid it.

Somewhere after the sidewalk ended and the dirt path veered down the mountain, the view of the valley opened before her. Amani began to dread seeing the asphalt spread down the valley. One day a big pile of rubble was dumped at the end of Seedo's driveway, and her father's. Vehicles with yellow license plates began to speed along the settlers' highway.

On her grandfather's mountaintop the Israelis built a road, dug holes, then put up sheds and trailers. Cars began to drive in and out, then a large shiny bus. Children wearing backpacks descended from it as if returning from a school elsewhere.

In the middle of the night, the bright lights on Seedo's Peak began to wake her. She stared out her window at the barbed wire fence. She rolled over, pulling the blankets over her head. She imagined taking her sheep up to the Firdoos, and slept.

After school she grazed the sheep in the olive grove, around the vineyards or the slope above her house. Soon not a blade of dry grass remained in the valley, and the sheep grew thinner.

Every time Amani took them to the water trough on the oasis, she hoped to escape to the Firdoos. Someone always stood behind the settlement fence above. Either the settlers kept a constant guard, or someone knew her habits. Either way, she couldn't risk being followed.

Her only hope was to take them in the dark.

The first Friday in October, Amani rose before the call to prayer to run across the valley. Every star had faded by the time she got the sheep onto the oasis, but to her relief it was too dim to make out anything on the mountaintop.

"*Yalla!*" she commanded, standing on top of the wall. "To the Firdoos."

Once again Sahem drove the animals toward her and

they obeyed, jumping onto the wall and over a few boulders before disappearing.

Heart pounding with excitement, Amani lifted Survivor onto the wall and crawled up and onto the path.

She looked over her shoulder frequently, glad when the dark shoulder of Seedo's Peak disappeared from view.

By the time she caught up with the flock beyond the Camel's Hump, the eastern sky was aglow with pink. On the plateau there was no trace of a road or fence. She drove the sheep straight for the craggy peak at the far end and climbed the rocky stairway from the fissure to the side of the balcony.

After weeks of dreaming about it, seeing the meadow again took her breath away. A shock of green in this dry, desolate place. She scanned it several times before motioning Sahem to bring up the sheep.

Sahem refused. He prowled around the bottom of the stairway, sniffing. He ran back to the sheep, barking his warning.

Amani guessed. The wolf had marked his territory.

"Sahem!" Amani commanded with her voice and the hand gesture. "Bring the sheep."

He wasn't happy about it, but he obeyed.

The flock headed immediately for the stream, then grazed hungrily, their heads nodding as they cropped the long, plentiful grass. Sahem was nervous, sniffing the air. If a lamb wandered away from the flock, he charged after it, barking furiously, insisting the animals stay together. Though the morning passed peacefully, he never relaxed his guard.

Amani pulled out the food she'd stuffed in her pocket. Tangy bites of cheese mixed with the sweet juice of grapes under her teeth. She sat on the balcony, enjoying every second of being here.

Seedo had done this. Lived in this beautiful place. Shared it with a wolf.

Throughout the day, her thoughts returned to the wolf. At school she'd studied Miss Aboushi's books on endangered animals. The wolf she'd seen resembled an Iranian wolf. What intrigued her most was seeing Seedo's viewpoint repeated in every book. Wolves in the wild did not prey upon humans. On the contrary, they would abandon a kill to avoid contact with the two-legged creature that had driven them from their territories, hunting them almost to extinction.

When the afternoon was almost over, Amani reluctantly gave Sahem the signal to herd the sheep down the stairway.

Something moved in her peripheral vision.

On his haunches, above the meadow, the wolf eyed her sheep. He was shockingly close. A streak of red blood across his muzzle helped Amani see him where he lay camouflaged among some rocks.

Amani edged her way back to the opening at the side of the balcony. His yellow eyes tracked her.

Shaken, Amani fled down the rocky stairs and drove the flock home.

NINETEEN

AT THE END OF SUPPER, Ammo Hani negotiated a deal over the phone. For three days the grape harvest had sat in crates in the back of the truck. There were no buyers in the city. Israeli checkpoints prevented them from reaching other markets. Another day and the fruit would be spoiled.

Smiling, Ammo Hani said goodbye and explained. The juice factory in the city would buy every last grape if they could bring them tonight.

"Who wants to come?"

For a few minutes Amani felt the happiness of child-hood. Nothing cheered the whole family like taking a harvest into Al Khalil. With Wardeh, she climbed eagerly into the space at the back of the truck. The smell of the grapes — too sweet before supper — now smelled like hope.

"Why let them control our lives?"

Amani tensed. An argument was brewing between Baba and Ammo Hani on the dark driveway.

"You know it's illegal for Palestinians to use their high-ways. All they have to do is look at the color of our license plate. If they stop us — "

"They'd stop us from breathing if they could. The grapes are too ripe. If we take the Road Through Hell, they'll burst their skins."

Baba's voice, coaxing. "We'll go slowly. They'll buy them…"

Murmuring. Too low to hear clearly. Then Ammo Hani yelling, "Get in! Don't worry, I won't go on their cursed highway. *Khalas.*"

The truck started up, jerked into motion and whined onto the village road.

After the village the truck turned left. Bounces now. They were on a tractor path. The truck idled, then turned sharply. No more bouncing. They were on a smooth surface. Like Wardeh opposite her, Amani leaned out the back of the truck to see where they were.

Ammo Hani was driving on the shoulder of the highway. Any second now he should cross over to the other side and take a route over the hills. Amani clutched the railing and leaned out farther to peer around the side of the truck. Darkness everywhere. Ammo Hani had turned off the headlights.

Amani's stomach tightened with fear. Did he mean to stay on the shoulder of the settlers' highway? How long?

Ammo Hani was speeding up, shifting gears. Voices rose and fell in the cab, the complaining engine drowning out the argument. The grade was slight but steady. No cars passed. If Ammo Hani stayed on the highway they'd arrive at the old gate into the city — blocked to Palestinian traffic. Did he think they could just park and unload the grapes unnoticed?

On Amani's left she glimpsed the big settlement above the valley. Lights. Orange tiled roofs among green trees. Then — wham! — the truck veered sharply to the left. Tires on an even smoother surface. The highway. Still turning sharply they bumped off the highway, tires back on the stony shoulder. Heading downhill.

Ammo Hani had turned around.

Amani stared up the dark highway behind them. Headlights sped toward them — one, two, three, four, five pairs of glowing eyes, growing larger, gaining quickly.

Amani's insides tumbled. Four army jeeps approached, passed them — each full of soldiers. Ammo Hani braked. Wardeh fell against her. The fifth jeep parked behind them, shining its headlights into the back of the truck.

A line of soldiers appeared, rifles pointed at them. Amani imagined a similar line at the front of the truck where they heard the order in Arabic.

"You! Driver! Out!"

The squeak of the driver's door as Ammo Hani stepped out.

Beside her, Wardeh groaned and shifted to see what was happening. Baba had told them a thousand times never to move if rifles were pointed at them. Amani clutched Wardeh's arm.

"Hands up. *Hawiyyeh*."

Then Ammo Hani's voice. Defiant. "How can I give you my papers with my hands up?"

Voices in Hebrew. A thud, like the sound of something hard on flesh. A groan. "What is in truck?"

Ammo Hani's voice. More defiant. "My family. We're taking our grapes to the juice factory in Al Khalil. Is it illegal to make juice?"

Words in Hebrew. The line of soldiers at the back of the truck stepped closer. The tip of a rifle approached her cousin, another Amani, and she nearly peed. She couldn't see the face behind it. Another soldier climbed up and shone a blinding light over their faces and the crates. Another climbed inside, grabbed the top crate and passed it out to waiting hands. Both soldiers jumped down. The crate was dumped onto the highway. Grapes spilled out, rolling in all directions.

More Hebrew.

The tips of the rifles retreated. The soldiers backed away.

Whoever was questioning Ammo Hani spoke again. "You have no license to travel on this highway."

"We weren't on your highway."

Another thud. Another groan.

It terrified Amani to hear her uncle being attacked. She

regretted every time she'd ever wished he didn't rule the family. They needed his strength and fierceness.

"You're breaking the law. This is a security zone. No Palestinians."

"This is an illegal occupation. This is Arab land."

"This is an Israeli highway. You —"

A cellphone rang. More Hebrew.

"You. Hands back."

More Hebrew. The sounds of a struggle. More thuds. Ammo Hani groaned.

Amma Fatima crawled toward the railing, crying out, "What are you doing to my husband? Hani?"

Wardeh joined her. "Baba!"

Confused, Sitti asked, "What's happening to Hani? Someone tell me what's happening."

Amani felt her cousin shaking violently and wrapped an arm around her. Before she could answer Sitti, they heard a horrible sound like something being dragged. Two soldiers walked behind the truck into the headlights, dragging a limp Ammo Hani by the armpits. A piece of white plastic bound his wrists behind his back. A sack covered his slumped head.

He was gone as quickly as he appeared, dragged from the circle of light. All Amani saw were the bouncing soles of his boots, grapes knocked wildly to one side, then nothing.

The slam of jeep doors startled her. Amma Fatima and

Wardeh screamed at the soldiers not to take him. Amani was quiet, focused on the sounds outside.

"*Yalla!*" a soldier yelled. "No Arab truck here. Go home."

The last few soldiers backed away. The jeeps roared off, their headlights growing smaller up the highway.

Baba ran after them, fists clenched in the air, yelling bad words Amani had never heard him say.

Back home, Baba told them over and over that the soldiers would take Hani to the prison inside the big settlement. He'd go first thing in the morning and find his brother. He pulled out his cellphone and began to make phone calls, pacing the garden. Amani helped Wardeh spread out five mattresses for them. Baba had parked the truck near the porch and the smell of grapes was sickeningly sweet. Amani wanted to ask Baba to move it but she'd never seen him so agitated. He chain-smoked, cursing between phone call after phone call.

If Wardeh or her mother cried or started talking about Ammo Hani, Sitti asked what was wrong and needed to be told again. Finally Amma Fatima spoke sharply to Sitti, "Don't ask again! Lie down. It's time to sleep."

It was the worst night Amani had ever known. She dozed through the first call to prayer, not waking until Wardeh shook her.

They were late for school.

TWENTY

"ALLAH HELPS THOSE WHO ARE PATIENT," Sitti said during the long hours, the slow days, the crawling weeks in which they waited for news of Ammo Hani.

Patience, Amani decided, comes to those who can forget.

At school Amani could not forget. Her friends all had a father or uncle, cousin or brother who'd spent months, sometimes years, in Israeli prisons. Amani listened to the stories of beatings, humiliation and no trials. They hated the Israelis and their prisons.

Something hard had taken root in Amani's heart. When the call to prayer sounded down the valley, she remembered how Seedo had prayed without anger in his heart.

If Allah saved her uncle she would sweep it out, and pray again.

Phone calls with Mama turned tense. Baba didn't want to worry her with what had happened. Amani wanted to say, Come home, Mama. We need you more than your mother does. No. She couldn't tell Mama how she wished Musical Sitti would die.

After Ammo Hani's disappearance, Baba made frequent visits to the prison inside the big settlement. Amani knew whenever he'd faced Israeli soldiers and settlers. She'd return from school and find him at home, staring at a book, smoking one cigarette after the other. The pages never turned.

It took a week to learn that Hani had been taken to a prison in the Negev. There was no hope of a trial.

"You said we could fight our battles in court!" Amani lashed out. "What's the point? Wouldn't you rather see him fight?"

The look on her father's face silenced her.

"No," he said. "It's not right how they take our land or Hani without a trial. I believe in non-violent means, even now."

But he was beginning to have the dried-out appearance of a piece of stale bread. How they needed Mama! She was their raisin. Wrinkled, yet plump with sweetness.

Amani couldn't pinpoint when Amma Fatima began to stay in bed or when Fatima's sister, Islah, began to visit from the village. Islah got Amma Fatima up, dressed and sitting in a sunny spot in her rose garden while Wardeh and Raja' scrubbed floors or dishes or laundry and prepared supper.

Islah would hold Fatima's hand and tell stories of their childhood. "Remember what our father used to say? The olive tree survives the long summer months without water by sending its roots down deep. We need to be like our olive trees."

When Mama phoned that night she had bad news. Musical Sitti had stopped eating and was in a coma.

"The Israelis took Ammo Hani. He's in prison," Amani blurted out. Baba glared at her. Amani couldn't stop. "Amma Fatima's sick. Islah has to come every day to get her out of bed. No one knows what's wrong with her. Baba's smoking all the time — "

Baba grabbed the phone. He walked away with it, and Amani watched him pace and gesture as he talked with Mama.

He'd scold her when he got off the phone, but she would not apologize. She was glad Mama knew. They needed her home.

He said goodbye. To Amani's surprise he was smiling. "It takes a woman to understand a woman. It might be just the thing to help Fatima."

The next day he took Amma Fatima to the prison with him. Mama said Fatima needed to conduct the search for her husband. She had to stop feeling helpless.

It worked. Not only did Amma Fatima come home and make dinner, she brought wonderful news. Hani was going to be released. He'd be home in a week.

Amani took the sheep to the oasis, her heart and step

lightened by the news. Losing Ammo Hani to prison had been terrible. Even if he was a tyrant he kept the family strong. They needed him back.

Ever since her one full day in the meadow, Amani had debated the risks of going back. Seedo had lived there a whole winter. Was she as brave as Seedo? When she filled the water trough and looked up to see someone behind the settlers' fence, she put off her decision for another day. The sheep crowded around her, bleating with hunger. They remembered the way to food. She remembered a pair of yellow eyes, tracking her sheep.

Instead she herded the flock down through the olive trees to the village road that dead-ended in a big pile of rubble in front of the settlers' highway. None of the villagers came this way anymore. She felt nervous grazing the sheep here, alone whenever an Israeli vehicle sped by. But the animals found something to nibble and they went farther each day, south along the shoulder of the highway.

October surrendered to November. In Canada Musical Sitti died and was buried. Mama was packing her bags to come home. Only twenty-four hours remained before Ammo Hani's return. Amma Fatima was her old self, pruning her rose bushes, baking Ammo Hani's favorite almond cookies, scouring her house and Sitti's.

After supper they sipped sweetened tea on the porch. Amma Fatima turned to Baba as the head of the family.

"What meat can we have tomorrow? I'd like to invite my sister's family to a feast."

Amani tensed. Ammo Hani liked nothing better than lamb.

"I'll kill a few chickens."

"What if they've beaten him?"

"Then we'll take care of him."

"How will he get home? He'll have no money for a taxi. You can't take the truck inside their gates."

Baba lit a cigarette. "I'll take two donkeys in the morning and bring him home."

The next morning Amani brought a small bit of milk to the kitchen door. Sitti sat by the bake oven, a toothless grin on her face.

"Amani!"

"Sitti? You remembered my name. Do you know who's coming home today?"

Sitti paused, her head turned to the kitchen.

"My brother, Hani, is coming home."

Baba appeared in the doorway, doubled over with laughter.

"He's your son, Mama," he laughed. "My brother. What does it matter? He's Hani! Hani is coming home. And so is my wife! Your mother." He beamed at Amani. "Think of the arguments we'll have again!"

"Where's your wife?" Sitti asked.

"In Canada."

"She was waiting for Sitti to die," Amani added.

"Die? Who says I'm going to die?"

"Not you, Mama," Baba said. "My wife's mother. Rose, my wife, will be home in a few days. Now," he said, sitting on the empty stool beside her. "It's time I taught you how you make the best bread in Palestine."

"You have to eat the one you make," Amani laughed, giving him a ball of dough. "She'll be home in time for the olive harvest, won't she?"

Baba nodded. His hands were like paddles, smacking the white ball.

Amani left them teasing each other and walked behind Wardeh and Raja' to school.

In the afternoon, she took the sheep to graze along the highway. Seedo's house disappeared from view. Amani wondered how far she dared to continue.

A small truck with several men seated in its open back drove by on the other side of the highway. They shook their fists at her and yelled, "Arab dog!"

Something about the insult, the laughing men, worried Amani enough to stop. She watched the truck for a long minute, longer, enough to notice it slow down. There were no other cars on the highway. No one anywhere.

She ran the sheep as hard as she could back onto the vil-

145

lage road. For once she was glad of the blockade. Ahead she saw the end of their vineyards and the olive terraces beside Seedo's house.

She glanced back. The truck was speeding away. Leaning on her crook, she cried with relief.

What was she thinking, taking the sheep that way, alone? It *was* dangerous. Ammo Hani had been right about so many things.

A delicious smell made her mouth suddenly water. Amma Fatima and Islah were roasting the chickens outside. Amani hurried to Sitti's kitchen to help. She carried bowls of rice and vegetables to the porch, listening for the sound of hooves trotting down the village road. The sun was setting. It would be dark soon.

Amma Fatima called out, "Meat's ready!"

Platters of succulent chicken were laid on a low table in the middle of the porch. They began to take their time, arranging cushions, lighting several kerosene lanterns.

"I'm cold!" Sitti complained. "Why are we eating out here?"

It was a good excuse to move everything inside to the salon. It was crowded with two long sofas and the TV, but they squeezed in together. They busied themselves, bringing chairs, pretending a patience no one felt.

The meat cooled. So did their excitement. Their voices turned anxious. Sharp.

Raja"s youngest sister, Uraib, whined, "I'm hungry. I don't want to wait."

"*Khalas!*" Amma Fatima shrieked, turning to Islah. "Keep her quiet."

The four-year-old hid in her mother's lap and began to cry. So did Amma Fatima. Wardeh wrapped her arms around her mother.

Amani rearranged the dishes.

Abu Nader prayed *Bism Allah* and nodded for them to begin.

"We'll eat slowly and save them plenty. It will make them come faster."

Sitti asked, "Who are we waiting for?"

Islah whispered, "Your sons."

The door clicked open. Amani hadn't heard the donkey over Uraib's crying. Cool air entered the room with Baba. He stood alone in the doorway. His face and shoulders sagged with fatigue.

"I'm sorry," Baba winced, taking in the feast, the circle of hopeful faces. "They made me wait all day before someone said he's not being released. No reason. There's no point going back until after Ramadan. They won't give us another release date for a month or two."

Amani picked at the cold food, wondering what Ammo Hani might be eating. Or not.

TWENTY-ONE

RAIN BEAT AGAINST THE CLASSROOM window. Amani watched the drops make random drip-slip bursts down the pane of glass.

Tomorrow was the last day of school before the break for olive harvest. If Mama's plane was on time, she had already landed in Jordan. Amani checked the clock. Mama might be across the border and the Allenby Bridge, already on her way to Ramallah.

"Soon it will be Ramadan," Miss Aboushi said. "I'm going to teach you games and songs in English."

The girls made approving sounds.

"And you're going to write poems."

Groans.

Miss Aboushi laughed. "Okay. How about this? I'll show you a game. And then you write a poem."

They agreed.

"This game is an easy card game called Go Fish." She held up a deck of cards, then fanned a few so they could see that the deck contained pictures of different animals.

"You need to learn their names in English and then you can play tomorrow."

Miss Aboushi handed out two lists and made them repeat the names after her. Then she explained the rules of the game.

"Can we play?"

"I said I'd show you the game. Tonight you must learn the vocabulary for homework. Tomorrow you can play. Now it's time for a poem."

More groans.

"A poem can play with a single word. I want you to start with a word about yourself or the world around you. For example...look outside."

She wrote a word on the board: precipitation.

"Does anyone know what pre-ci-pi-ta-tion means?"

Amani knew, but kept quiet.

"Pre-ci-pi-ta-tion. No one knows? Precipitation means all the forms of water that fall from the sky."

"Like rain?" asked Souad.

"Yes. Good. I'll write all your words down. What else?"

More hands shot up.

"Snow."

"Hail."

"Now play with that word. What does it make you think of next? Anything!"

"Umbrella."

"Hot milk."

"Red boots."

"You've got the idea. We've studied some of Rumi's poems. I want you to start with your name and let any words or images follow. During Ramadan you'll memorize your poems to recite to the class."

Amani thought of her birth story. A poem came quickly.

My name, Amani, means wishes
but I have only one.
The night I was born
my grandfather told my mother
that a walk up the mountain
was Allah's way of
precipitating a birth.
She climbed the sheep path
to the peak above his house.
I fell from her body — free
as rain through sky.
My name, Amani, means wishes
but I have only one.
My blood is mixed with
the soil of our land
and I will never leave.

Writing the poem made Amani feel better. Walking home she heard the afternoon call to prayer, and Seedo's voice. *Sweep out anger from your heart.*

I can't, she answered. She held out her arms like an olive tree, inviting the rain to wash away what it could.

Across the highway Seedo's house was strangely dark and quiet. Baba stood on the porch and waved. She ran to meet him.

He lit a cigarette and told her how he'd returned at noon to find the house empty, Sitti missing. Fatima was at home in bed, her back to the world, unable to rouse herself. He'd found his mother wandering the village road, lost and shivering.

"I took Sitti to Islah's house in the village. Then I came back for Fatima and their things. Islah can manage more easily if they're with her in the village. My mother was so happy to have little children around her."

Baba stared across the valley. Wardeh was crossing the highway under an umbrella.

"They'll be happy in the village," Amani said. "Not me. We can't let the settlers think we've abandoned our homes. And how could I tend the sheep?"

Baba nodded. "I'll take Wardeh into the village and bring back supper to our house. Mama's plane was late. She'll call us tomorrow."

In the sheep pen Amani slipped Seedo's old plastic poncho over her head. The heavy rain turned to a light drizzle. On the oasis the sheep bleated, hungry for the meadow. It was hard to see clearly through the rain. Today she would risk it.

Steep and slippery, the path up and around the slope was hard to climb. Amani lifted her poncho, watching the ground for a secure foothold.

Beyond the Camel's Hump she was shocked at how different the plateau looked in the rain. Lonely. Unfriendly. How had Seedo survived a whole winter here? Were those peaks or storm clouds behind the curtain of rain?

Amani's steps slowed. Getting lost here would be dangerous. She had no blanket, food, matches or knife. Behind her, the Camel's Hump was quickly obscured by rain.

Sahem barked and ran ahead confidently. He knew the way. Even so, Amani was relieved when she saw the pileup of boulders on the rugged slope.

Seedo had shared the Firdoos with a wolf. Why couldn't she?

The sheep rushed past, driven by two simple needs: water and food. Their woolly backs protected them from the cold rain.

Amani huddled under the poncho, wiggling her toes inside her rubber boots. She walked back and forth across the meadow to keep warm, eyeing the slopes constantly.

Would the wolf appear? Would he be hungry? They picked the weakest, the old or a stray.

A rock high above the meadow seemed to move. Amani's mouth went dry. Sahem barked at the sheep, driving them quickly off the meadow.

A lone wolf trotted through the curtain of rain, head up. When he neared the edge of the meadow he slowed. She saw his hesitation. Did he see hers?

"You can't have one," she yelled.

His tail shot up. So did his ears. Alert. Eyeing her. Amani stayed absolutely still. His paws were large. His coat had thickened. Rain dripped from it, unnoticed.

Then his gaze shifted to the stairway. His ears flattened. Lips curled to show his teeth. His tail shot straight out behind him.

Amani turned. Saw nothing at the stairway. Turned back. The wolf was running away. Up the slope. Sure-footed and lean, his heels didn't touch the ground. He ran faster than Amani thought possible, blending into the rain.

Something had scared him off.

Crook raised to protect herself, Amani crept toward the opening in the boulders.

Below her, the rocky stairway was empty. Below it, Sahem guarded the sheep.

There, across the plateau, she saw him. Just in time.

Almost out of sight, a two-legged figure in blue jeans was moving quickly, then like the wolf, disappeared into the rain.

The settler boy was running away. From what?

Puzzled, she ordered Sahem to start driving the sheep home. Heading down the slippery stairway, Amani put one hand on the rocks to steady herself. Something small and white lay tucked under a ledge. She bent forward, reaching for it. Her eyes widened.

The wild carrot blossoms she'd dropped two months ago had been carefully dried, tied with long blades of grass into a bow, placed in a clear plastic bag and tucked under the overhanging rocks to keep dry.

The settler's son had brought her a gift.

TWENTY-TWO

THE FALL RAINS, SEEDO ALWAYS SAID, were Allah's way of washing the olive trees to make the harvest easier.

School was closed for a few days so students could celebrate the olive harvest. Amani ran home, hoping Omar and Mama had arrived while she'd been at school. Last night Mama had phoned to say the line-up to cross the border was impossibly long. She had to return to Amman.

Shivering, breathless, Amani flung open the side door. The house was quiet. She walked by Baba's desk, still empty, and to her room where she changed into dry clothes. Only the Israeli border separated her from her mother now, not an ocean. Soon, she told herself. They'd be home soon.

By the time Amani reached the sheep pen the sun was out. Even so, she stuffed matches, a knife and the poncho into a small knapsack before letting the sheep out. On the oasis she didn't bother glancing up at the fence. If anyone stood there, it would be that boy. After yesterday, she'd decided not to worry about him.

She climbed the stairway and immediately spotted the wolf high above the meadow. She hesitated.

The sheep shoved past her, thirsty for the stream. Sahem sniffed the air. His eyes found the wolf, too, and he chased after the sheep, barking furiously.

The wolf stretched out on the ground like a sphinx, observing them intently.

A stand-off. She assessed the situation. He hadn't come any closer. He was alone. And her sheep were hungry.

Amani opened her crook like a gate and let the sheep rush onto the meadow. Sahem charged past. No. They were not going to the other end of the meadow. They had to stay together.

Amani spread her poncho over a boulder and leaned against it. The sheep cropped hungrily, filling their stomachs.

Time passed. Maybe an hour.

Amani had just decided the wolf had fallen asleep when he moved. He'd smelled or seen something she had not. He trotted uphill and disappeared.

Amani ran past the sheep to the rocky stairs, an angry growl in her throat.

A scraping sound below. From the ledge on the left.

Amani jumped down to be level with the ledge. The boy stood flattened against the wall as if willing himself to become part of the rocky balcony.

He wasn't as old as Omar, but older than her. His

longish hair made it hard to pinpoint his age. Red pimples nearly hid his good looks. Black binoculars hovered in one hand like a weapon, the same way she was holding out her crook. His eyes were wary.

"I came to watch the wolf," he said. "I didn't come to hurt you."

His English was exactly like Miss Aboushi's. Amani remembered the flowers, and how he'd run away yesterday.

Still, he had no business following her into the Firdoos.

She made two circles with her hands, placed them over her eyes, pointed to the binoculars, then to herself.

"My binoculars? You want to try my binoculars?" He hesitated, then held them out. "They're good ones. They were a gift from my grandparents for my bar mitzvah."

He took a step toward Amani and let her take them.

She'd understood almost every word.

She trained the binoculars on the boy's blurred face and brought his eyes into focus. They were dark brown with flecks of gold and green.

"I'm a bird-watcher," he said.

She focused on his moving lips.

"Only now I'm a wolf-watcher." He smiled. Metal braces covered his teeth. "It's amazing to see a wolf in the wild. There's a protected pack up in the Golan Heights, but he's not one of those. I think he's an Iranian wolf. They're endangered, you know."

Amani followed most of what he said. She trained the binoculars on him, silent. It seemed to make him talk.

"It's rude to stare like that, you know. I wanted to meet you yesterday but…you looked so angry."

He paused, giving her an opportunity to say something. She kept her face impassive. He continued. "I guess I'd be angry, too, if I were you. I'm here because of my father. It's been his dream to build a settlement. My mom refused to come, but I was curious. Everything changed the first day I saw you. You and that wolf. I never expected that. To feel we were chasing you off your land. I can't get near him, you know. I have to watch from down here. There's a hole between the boulders. If I go on the meadow, he disappears. You're freaking me out a little. You can give back my binoculars any time. Like now. Or now. My dad will be pissed off if I lose them. Not that it matters. We've been arguing since that day. I can't stand the talk in the settlement. I want to go back to New York and live with my mom. Rethink how to make *aliya*. So yeah, hey, keep my binoculars."

Immediately, Amani thrust the binoculars toward him.

His eyes narrowed. "You understand me, don't you."

She narrowed her eyes, mimicking him. "Yes."

He grinned. His face lit up. "That's fantastic. Why didn't you say so?"

"You a settler. Settlers do bad things."

He stopped smiling. "We do bad things? You're the ones who do bad things. You don't recognize our country. You come into our towns with your suicide bombers. You kill innocent people. Women. Children in schools."

"I don't kill. I am a shepherd."

"Not you," he said, his voice losing its anger. "Of course, I don't mean you. I mean Palestinians. I mean terrorists."

"I am no terrorist. My family is no terrorist. You steal our land. You put my Ammo Hani in prison. You make us hate you. We fight Israel."

He looked appalled. "God gave us this land. This is *haeretz*. Our holy land. I wish it didn't have to be this way, but it is. You should leave. Who did you say is in prison?"

Amani couldn't remember the English word for uncle. There was so much she was angry about. Now that she'd started there was no stopping.

"You put fence around the mountain of my grandfather. My sheep need this mountain. You dig up our grapes to make highway for you. Only you. You don't ask. You take. Your father kill my sheep. Your father have gun. I have no gun."

Something happened in his eyes. "I tried to stop him. He says you're all dangerous and that we have to defend ourselves. He's afraid of you. He's trying to scare you away. You should go before anyone gets hurt."

At the top of the rocky stairway Sahem barked at her. Was it time to go home?

Amani didn't want to be angry. Not in the Firdoos. She didn't want to talk to this settler boy anymore.

"Okay. I go away now."

She gave the hand signal. The sheep charged past her, down the steps and onto the plateau where they spread out to graze. Amani turned her back on the boy and stormed down the steps.

"No!" he called. "I didn't mean you. Don't go."

They would never understand each other. Never. Amani kept moving.

"Please, before you go, at least...tell me your name?"

Amani stopped. She turned and glared at him.

"Palestine."

He rolled his eyes. "I know that's not your real name." He managed to smile, though, which amazed Amani.

"Okay, Palestine. Mine's Jonathan. It's good to meet you finally. Here, in this beautiful place. You have no idea how much I've wanted to come back. I was worried someone would see me and find that path. Could we try again?"

Amani nodded. "Okay, Jonathan. I'll meet you here after the olive harvest. I don't have time until then."

TWENTY-THREE

BABA'S PHONE RANG. He pressed a tiny button marked Talk.

"Marhaba, habibti!" he shouted. He motioned for Amani to stop chopping. Amani swept the diced tomatoes into a bowl and followed him out of the kitchen. It was Mama.

The look on his face altered quickly. He sank onto the edge of the sofa, leaning his head against his free hand as he listened.

"I'll go to the permit office in Al Khalil. You go back to the border tomorrow. Go back every day. Call me and let me know."

He snapped the phone shut. "They denied her entry."

Amani sank onto the sofa.

Baba lit a cigarette and began to pace the length of the house.

"What about Omar?" Amani asked.

"He's waiting for her in Ramallah. We'll get her home somehow. Then she's never leaving the valley again."

"I've been counting the days," Amani said. "I even wanted my grandmother to die — "

"Khalas," he said, pulling her close "Don't say that. You didn't really. You wanted Mama home. I felt the same thing. What did Seedo always say if a ewe went missing?"

Amani forced a smile. "Find her and bring her back."

"So. I have to make some phone calls," Baba said.

Mama and Omar were not going to walk in the door. They would not be home for the olive harvest. Where did Baba find his patience?

She heard sounds outside. Voices came from across the valley. Worried, Amani stared at Baba. He was preoccupied, talking on the phone in Hebrew, pacing.

She went out the side door, closing it behind her so she could see across the dark valley. On Seedo's Peak the lights of the settlement blazed. Nothing moved on the slope below the fence. Seedo's house was dark. So was Ammo Hani's beside it.

As she stared though, a light went on inside it. A few seconds later a man approached the steps of Seedo's porch holding a lantern, carrying a small child on his hip. He stopped partway up the steps. Voices again, calling to each other in Arabic. A girl ran up the steps and took the child from the man. A small, stooped woman, wearing a long dress and hijab climbed slowly behind her.

"Sitti!" Amani cried, recognizing her grandmother.

The people on the porch turned and waved.

"Amani? Where are you?" Raja"s voice. She was the girl on the steps, holding her little sister, Uraib.

"Over here! My house." Amani opened the door so she stood in the light.

"We've brought food and family. Even your cousin, Nahla, from the city." Abu Nader's voice boomed across the narrow valley. "We've come to help with the olive harvest tomorrow. Where's your father?"

Soon Amani sat beside Baba, enjoying a noisy meal on Seedo's porch. It felt like old times. Amani's older cousins and their families made the family circle large and warm. Surrounded by her daughters, Amma Fatima managed to smile. Baba told them about Mama's trouble, and there was a long discussion about how to get her home from Jordan. At one point, Wardeh reached out to hold Amani's hand.

"May Allah keep her safe," Wardeh said.

"And your father, too," Amani said, meaning it.

After supper they packed up the leftovers for their picnic the next day. Where were the ladders? What about the plastic sheets? Buckets and canvas sacks? Ammo Hani had neatly stored everything in the back of the cave.

Finally everything was ready. It was too cold to sleep outdoors. They divided among the three houses, agreeing that the olive harvest would begin at dawn.

First to rise, Amani went quietly to milk the sheep. She

took the animals up to the oasis to drink and eat whatever they could nibble, listening for harvesters among the upper row of trees. The sun turned the sky pink, warming the air. The olive grove remained quiet.

Amani sat on the wall, resisting the pull of the hidden path. It was strong, but the pull of the olive harvest was just as strong. She tapped her feet. Where was her family? Something must have happened. Worried, she drove the sheep back to the pen, and saw people among the trees at the bottom of the hill. She hadn't heard their voices from the oasis.

Baba was picking from a ladder when Amani joined them.

"Why didn't you start at the top?" she asked.

Her cousins' young children swarmed the trees like monkeys, looking for the hidden fruit on the small outer branches.

"The settlers can't see us down here," Baba answered. "As your mother liked to say, a little distance can be a good thing."

With the early start and so many working together, they picked sixteen trees the first day. They set up the equipment under a row in the middle of the terraces for the second day. Their backs ached and their fingers were numb. Amani brought yogurt and cheese from the cave, pleased she had something to feed everyone.

Early the next morning after watering the animals, she met Abu Nader on his way to the olive orchard.

"Where do you graze them now?" he asked, eyeing her flock. The Firdoos had fattened them a little and given them more energy.

Caught off guard, Amani pretended to have trouble closing the gate.

"Wherever I can."

He sighed. "Years ago my flock was nearly as large as your grandfather's. Now I have a ram and two lambs and we'll eat one, maybe both, before Ramadan ends. Your grandfather would be proud of you. Even a fool can see you are the shepherd's granddaughter."

Amani let Abu Nader's praise strengthen her throughout the long day of picking. Raja''s clear singing voice helped, too. Someone would call out a song, and Raja' would sing a verse before they all joined in. Singing lifted everyone's spirits and made it easier to ignore complaining muscles.

They picked more slowly than the first day, but steadily. Two trees before breakfast, another six before they reached the upper terraces. The barbed wire on the fence around Seedo's Peak became visible. No one called out for a song. Silently, they stopped work for a late lunch.

Stomachs full, all but the youngest children and Sitti lay on the ground to ease their aching backs, then set to work again. A few hours of daylight remained. Amani wasn't the only one who glanced at the fence frequently.

Then a dog bayed loudly from Seedo's Peak. More dogs. Angry voices.

Amani twisted sharply to stare at the fence. Settlers were steadily gathering behind the chain-link — women, children, a few men holding rifles, dogs running back and forth.

They began to shout, "Go away! This is our land!"

Amani looked for Jonathan. He wasn't there. Several men appeared around the western edge of the peak. Below the fence. Coming fast. Rifles slung over their shoulders, they reached the narrow sheep track that switchbacked down the upper face of the mountain, and began a sliding, running descent. Someone fired a shot over the olive trees.

Terrified, Amani gripped the ladder she was picking from and tried to climb down. Her foot missed the rung.

Baba yelled, "*Rouh!* Take the children."

Everyone was running, shouting.

Amani leapt off the ladder and ducked under the tree. Nahla's eldest, Samir, clung to a branch, hiding.

Amani held out her arms. "*Yalla!* Climb on my back. I'll carry you to your mother."

"They'll shoot me."

"No, they won't," she promised. Then she realized he was right. If Samir climbed on her back, he'd be a target.

"Have you ever seen a picture of a kangaroo?"

Samir nodded.

"So you're going to ride in front. Can you do that? Can you pretend you're a kangaroo?" His face brightened and he slipped down, arms tight around her neck, legs behind her waist.

Amani ran, the last one, down through the terraces, past the sheep pen and through the rose garden. She leaned against the porch and let Samir scramble off into his mother's outstretched arms.

Two army jeeps were parked in the driveway. Baba was talking to an Israeli soldier. Amani's heart sank. It was the short officer they'd angered at the protest over the highway. Amani desperately wished the rabbi were here.

"You're too close to the settlement. Stay out of the olive trees," the officer said.

Baba tried to reason with him. It was their family's land. They were peaceful farmers, picking their harvest.

A shout from the olive grove captured everyone's attention.

Three settlers walked toward them, pointing their rifles at the family on the porch. One approached the officer and addressed him in Hebrew, making angry gestures at the peak, the grove, Baba and the family on the porch. The officer looked constantly from Baba to the settler, his face stern. Finally he nodded and said something too quiet for

Amani to hear. Whatever it was, Baba didn't like it. He raised his hands in the air, a pleading gesture, and Amani clearly heard, "…what right do you have?"

The officer yelled, "Our security. It gives us every right."

The settler exchanged a few more words with the officer, then strode back through the garden, motioning his companions to follow. They paused by the sheep pen and stared at her flock.

Amani turned cold. To her relief, they moved into the olive grove and were gone.

In a loud voice, the officer directed his next comments at all of them on the porch. "Don't step foot in that orchard again or I'll confiscate your truck, everything you have. The settlers are afraid you'll hide snipers behind the trees and try to shoot at them. You're too close to the settlement. You should move to the village."

Baba watched the soldiers drive away. A vein bulged at the side of his neck. He paced into the garden and back, raking his hands through his hair before he said, "Go home. The settlers will shoot if they see us in the olive grove. The army will protect them, not us, even if we're killed picking fruit, unarmed, in our own orchard."

The adults talked for a long time but Amani didn't listen. It was hard to believe. Not allowed in the olive orchard? The more she thought about it the angrier she felt.

An arm slid around her shoulder. Wardeh and her sisters had formed a circle around her.

"Come to the village with us, Amani. Please. It's not safe to stay close to the settlement tonight. You can bring your sheep to my uncle's pen. Abu Nader would love you to tend his sheep with yours."

Wardeh's offer nearly made her cry. Wardeh had included her sheep. But there was nothing for nine more sheep to eat in the village.

Amani searched for the right words.

"Thank you. Give me a little time. You're like sisters to me."

On the driveway Baba helped Sitti into the wagon. Her cousins climbed in and took their places. Amani stood beside her father. They waved as the wagon jostled and bumped onto the old village road, getting smaller. The sun was about to set and the sky was red, the air cold.

Baba said, "Keep waving. The settlers are watching everything we're doing. Imagine you're up there watching us. What do you see? All but two of the dangerous Palestinian terrorists have left."

Amani waved and imagined watching herself. What was Baba planning?

"So now we walk in front of Seedo's house where they can't see us. Here's my plan. The truck's partly loaded at the bottom of the olive grove. It will be dark soon and when it is, I'll get the last sacks under the trees and load them onto the truck. I can't risk the checkpoint outside Al Khalil. That officer will have my name on a list. He'd love to see me join my brother. I'll drive the truck to Bethlehem. You can ride the donkey and take the sheep into the village — "

"No, Baba. I'm going to help you."

If Omar or Ammo Hani were here, the men would work together to save the harvest. They wouldn't be afraid.

"You need the donkey to carry the heavy sacks," Amani said. "And I have a way with animals. I'll keep the donkey quiet."

"You're a brave girl, Amani. What would I do without you?"

When night fell, Amani's courage left with the light. The settlers would shoot if they saw anyone in the olive orchard. A nest of scorpions moved inside Amani's stomach. The only good thing about darkness was that she could hide her fear from Baba.

TWENTY-FOUR

BABA KNEW EXACTLY WHERE he'd left the bulging sacks in the last row they had picked after lunch. Like a bat he led Amani and the donkey through the dark orchard, not needing a flashlight.

If settlers came down the slope to confront them they would carry lights, wouldn't they? Amani watched for a telltale flicker as Baba heaved the sacks onto the donkey's back.

A sound — something moving over stones — made her jump. She stared at the dark trees. Were those branches? Or the long barrels of rifles, pointing at them?

"What was that?" she whispered.

"Not a settler," Baba whispered back. "Go wait for me in the truck."

Walk alone through the terraces?

"No. I'm keeping the donkey quiet."

She clung to the donkey's neck and followed Baba to the last sack, thanking the donkey for staying calm. Finished, they headed slowly down to the truck, too slowly for Amani's stomach. She ran to the passenger side and

171

threw up as quietly as she could. If Baba heard, he didn't say anything.

Night continued to hide them on the long drive to Bethlehem. Baba kept the headlights off. A sky full of stars and a half-moon cast an eerie glow over the land. They followed the village road past the grape fields to its dead-end at the settlers' highway. Amani clutched Baba's arm. She saw again the horrible image of Ammo Hani's boots disappearing, grapes rolling.

"Let go, Amani. I can't think or drive with you grabbing my arm. I know what you're thinking. We're not going on the highway. Relax."

"We're heading south. Isn't Bethlehem north?"

"It's not what you'd call a direct route," Baba said, and swung the wheel hard. They began to bounce over rough ground.

"But, Baba, it's all mountains and desert ahead."

"This is no time for a geography lesson. There are passes and valleys and old roads. Trust me on this, Amani. I know the way to Bethlehem."

Baba changed gears until he couldn't. The truck whined as they attacked the slope at a steep angle.

"Should I get out and walk?" Amani asked.

"Can you carry twenty sacks of olives?" Baba teased. "Stop worrying or I'll take you home. I used to bring Mama this way when she celebrated Christmas in Bethlehem."

"When was that?"

"Before the Separation Wall and the checkpoints made it feel like a prison."

"So how do we get in?"

"The back door."

His cellphone rang.

"We were just talking about you. What happened?"

He listened, shaking his head. "Amani's here with me. You tell her."

Amani took the phone. Mama explained how a soldier at the border had accused her of having a dangerous look and refused her entry.

"What did you do?"

"I nearly slapped her face," Mama continued. "She was young and pretty, like Raja'. Perhaps I did have a dangerous look. Tomorrow I'll wear makeup and a short dress and line up in front of a male soldier. I'll smile at him like crazy." Mama laughed. "If he can't see too well, I'll be home by dark."

"You don't have a short dress."

"I'm hemming one now."

They said goodnight. Amani gave up trying to understand where they were and gave in to the warmth of the cab and the rocking. She slept until Baba rolled down his window to ask for directions to the olive press. Cold night air jolted her awake. They were driving on narrow roads between low buildings. Amani caught glimpses of an enormous wall. Barbed wire. Glaring lights.

Bethlehem.

In spite of the late hour, there was a line of families and bulging bags outside the olive press. Amani helped Baba unload theirs at the end of the line. They were strangers here, but it didn't take Baba long to know everyone. When they heard his story someone brought a tray of coffee, another bread and fellafel. Several women surrounded Amani and asked about her uncle and Mama and the settlement. The line became a large circle, everyone eating, talking loudly above the noisy machines inside. Everyone had a story of a husband, son, brother or cousin who'd been in an Israeli prison, or someone who wasn't allowed to cross the border.

Someone suggested that Baba didn't have much time. He needed to drive home under cover of darkness. Everyone let them move to the head of the line.

Baba sold most of the oil for a fair price, keeping two containers for the family. He hummed the whole ride back, even on the bumpy descent into the valley. Amani peered out the window anxiously. A silvery mist blanketed the valley bed. She didn't relax until Baba parked beside Seedo's house and turned off the headlights.

They put one of the plastic containers in the cave.

"Something's wrong, Baba. Listen," Amani said. The

sheep had heard them arrive and were bleating from two days of hunger in the pen. From the other side of Ammo Hani's house the rooster was waking up the hens.

Baba looked at his watch. "There's no call to prayer. Strange for the first day of Ramadan."

Maybe the muezzin was sick? Amani listened to the sheep's pitiful bleating. They'd be sick, too, if they didn't fill their bellies.

"Isn't it too late for breakfast?" she asked, following Baba into Sitti's kitchen.

"The sun hasn't risen yet." Baba filled a small coffee pot with water and set it on a burner. "Are you in a hurry? There's no school today, is there?"

"No. But I need to take the sheep out. They're starving."

"We will be, too, if we don't eat something. I'm going to drive the other container of oil to Islah. Where will you graze the sheep?"

"A spot Seedo showed me for emergencies."

Baba yawned, too tired to ask more.

Amani set out leftovers while Baba made their coffee. She swallowed a bit of stale bread and a cold boiled egg. The first day of fasting would be hard. She ate, knowing it had to sustain her until sundown.

She ran to the pen, waiting to hear—finally!—the truck rumble away.

Yalla! She opened the gate, weighing the risks. A settler at the fence wouldn't be able to see them in the olive grove for the mist. But he'd hear them. They'd have to be quick and quiet.

The smell of the damp trees, the last rows heavy with unpicked fruit, angered her. From her anger she drew courage.

The sheep were neither quick nor quiet. They were weak with hunger and moved slowly through the upper terraces, bleating. Sahem barked. The sounds disturbed the early morning quiet.

Hurry, her spirit voice urged them. She ran ahead, guessing a spot on the wall near the hidden path, the sheep behind her.

To the Firdoos!

TWENTY-FIVE

A COLD WIND SWEPT OVER THE PLATEAU, swirling bits of loose dirt. Amani walked slowly, Survivor nudging her calf.

Amani patted the black forehead. "We're almost there. I'm too tired to carry you."

They climbed the last rugged steps up the balcony, and there it was. The small meadow. No wolf in sight.

Sahem relaxed and let the flock graze at the far end. It was a good sign.

Amani curled up in the grass, her crook at her side. She was so tired. Shielded from the cold wind by the balcony, the rising sun warmed the pocket of air above the meadow.

Two days of hard picking, followed by the night in Bethlehem had taken their toll. Amani fell asleep.

The sun was well across the sky when she woke. Sahem was barking. He'd corralled the sheep around the opening at the other end and was driving them off the Firdoos. Amani jumped to her feet, anxiously searching the slope.

Crouching low to the ground, two adult wolves

approached stealthily, heading for the meadow. Two half-grown pups followed. Thankfully the wind had shifted, sweeping off the slope. Sahem had caught their scent first.

Whatever the plan had been, the lead wolf suddenly changed his mind. Partner and pups obeyed immediately. A gray line of wolves angled up and over the rocky slope.

Jonathan stood in the opening above the stairway. He was pointing up the mountain where the wolves had just been. His face was a mixture of fear and awe.

"That was incredible," he said. "Did you see how quickly they moved as a pack?"

"You scared them. And me."

Jonathan tilted his head to one side and gave her a puzzled look.

"Is that some kind of thank you? Your sheep were nearly the dinner special."

He was teasing. What was it about boys and teasing? Amani picked up her crook and hurried toward the stairway.

"I need to take my sheep home."

"There are two of us. And your dog. They're afraid of humans, you know."

They walked in silence until they reached the Camel's Hump. There was plenty of light still. Jonathan surveyed the slope ahead and the plateau behind with his binoculars.

"Safe," he said.

Amani let the flock move onto the path down through the boulders. She followed, single-file, feeling Jonathan's eyes on her back.

"I've never seen the wolf children before," she said, feeling uncomfortable. "What is the word in English?"

"Pups. Are you learning English at school? It's awfully good. I learned Hebrew at religious school in New York but it's really awful."

"Awful? Good? Please, more slowly."

"Do…you…go…to…school?" Loud, staccato words.

What? Did he think she was stupid? Deaf?

"Yes…I…do."

He laughed. "Sorry. Let me try that again. It's hard to have a conversation with your back. Awful means bad. But when you put it with good, it means great. You must have an awfully good teacher."

"Miss Aboushi. She is Palestinian but grew up in America. Yes, she is awfully good."

"I learned Hebrew by reading the Torah. I can read a prayer but I can't take a bus to Tel Aviv."

Ahead of them, the sheep had reached the end of the path above the wall.

"Miss Aboushi says everyone in America plays Go Fish. Do you?"

Jonathan laughed. "When I was little I used to play it

all the time. My mom's a teacher in New York. She's big on educational games like that. I had a deck with trees."

Trees. A vivid image of armed settlers chasing her family from the olive grove made Amani swing around, fists clenched.

Jonathan took one look at her face and raised his hands in self-defense.

"What? What did I say?"

"Yesterday your people yelled at us. You bring dogs and guns. You bring your army. You don't let us pick our *zaytoon*."

"Yesterday?" Jonathan's voice rose, struggling to understand. "You mean what happened in the olive orchard? I wish you'd stop saying *you*. I wasn't there. I had a huge fight with my father because I tried to stop them. Taking the land this way feels wrong."

"We will fight you. We fight for our olive trees. Fight for our land."

Jonathan's face scrunched up. "You don't have to fight me. I know you love this land. But the settlers believe God gave them this land. They won't share *haeretz*. Don't fight them. The Israeli army has to protect them. It will only go badly for you."

Amani held up an imaginary rifle. "Your God says kill us? Steal our land?"

"They don't see it as stealing. They'll provoke you, kill

you if that's what it takes to get back their Holy Land. They plan to move the fence. I can't stop them. I'm sixteen. They don't listen to me."

Amani shook her fist. "Who will they listen to? Not me. You! You must tell them!"

Behind her, the sheep bleated impatiently. Sahem barked.

Amani turned in time to see Nasty bound out of the path, jump off the wall and charge up the oasis toward the water trough. The rest of the flock followed, Sahem chasing after them. Only Survivor waited for the shepherd.

Amani hoisted the lamb out of the path and scrambled down the boulders with Survivor to the top of the wall.

Half of Amani was back in the argument with Jonathan. Half of her watched Survivor follow the flock. The sheep crowded around the small trough, Sahem barking, barking, barking for Amani to come.

Something was wrong.

Amani focused all her attention on the scene around the trough, suddenly afraid.

Her shepherding instincts screamed, *Hurry*.

Small, turquoise plastic pellets lay under her pounding feet, scattered all over the oasis. Where had they come from? Who put water in the trough? She hadn't filled it this morning.

A strange powdery sediment lay at the bottom.

She wielded her crook, trying to drive the animals away.

"Khalas!" she yelled. She pushed her way in and threw her weight against the trough. It rocked slightly. A few waves sloshed over the sides.

Jonathan was a few seconds behind her. He ran to the other side, yelling, "It's too heavy. Help me push from this side. It's on a downhill slope."

She shoved her way through the sheep until she was beside Jonathan, their shoulders against the trough. They rocked it until it fell over. Water sloshed everywhere, soaking the ground. The sheep scattered, heads lowered, beginning the search for food.

Oh, no. Amani stared at them in dismay. How much had they drunk? What were they eating?

"The blue things. Don't let them eat!"

Swinging her crook she drove the sheep off the oasis and into the olive grove, Sahem and Jonathan helping her on either side.

Under the olive trees there were no pellets on the ground. Jonathan stopped in the first row of olive trees.

"None of you are safe," he said, his voice thick. "They don't want you close to the settlement. They want your water and your land. I can't believe they did that. I'm sick of what they're doing."

Amani didn't know the English word for poison, and she was too worried to speak.

"I can't go any farther," he said, obviously torn. "They could be watching. If I disappear into your olive grove, they'll come with their rifles."

Amani nodded. "I need to help my sheep."

Neither of them could voice the truth. If the water had been poisoned, it was already coursing through the sheep's bodies. Amani ran to find Baba. She needed his phone. She'd call the government vet, even though a voice in her head guessed what he'd say.

It was too late. Not even Allah could save her sheep now.

TWENTY-SIX

SEVERAL HOURS WENT BY before Amani reached the vet on Baba's cellphone. The sheep were unusually quiet, the only change she could report to him.

"You have no way of knowing what it was or how concentrated or how much each animal ingested," the vet warned. "Leave lots of fresh water for them. There's nothing you can do at this point but wait forty-eight hours."

Baba helped her carry buckets from the well to the pen. Baba insisted they go home for the night, and it was Baba who woke Amani the next morning, his face ashen.

Nasty and five of the sheep had died during the night.

"Which ones?" Amani asked, already crying as she crossed the strangely quiet valley. There was no call to prayer again. No sheep bleating to be let out. Beside her, Baba shook his head, not knowing their names.

What did it matter? She loved them all.

The dead sheep lay where they'd fallen in the night, limbs stiff. Flies swarmed. Romania stood motionless, diarrhea staining her rear end. Beside the gate, waiting for Amani, Survivor huddled beside another lamb. Their voices were thin wails. Amani's heart broke at the sight.

She flung open the gate and knelt, hugging the two lambs close to her.

She tried to imagine what Seedo might say. "You're scared of their dead bodies. We'll take them out, and you'll forget. It's going to be all right."

The lambs followed her and Baba to the well. Romania was too sick to move or drink when they set fresh water in front of her. Amani hugged her gently. Romania's eyes were glazed and she didn't respond.

Amani led the two lambs into the milking stall and closed it off to give them a little distance. She piled scraps of wood and tin high enough to block off the sight of the dead and the dying. By the time she returned to the main area of the pen, Romania lay on her side, her breathing faint. Amani knelt beside her.

The strong, sturdy ewe began to shake.

"A convulsion," Baba murmured.

Amani laid her hand on Romania's white back. When the shaking ended, it did so abruptly.

"She was the best ewe we ever had," Amani said, trying not to cry. "Her lambs were strong and healthy and she was a good mother."

Amani's fingers were deep in the knotted coat. She let

go slowly, her skin moist and smelling of spicy lanolin from the wool. She hid her face in her hands and wept.

Baba waited, saying nothing, giving her time.

The faint bleating of the lambs reminded her there was work to do. She wiped her eyes and stood.

"The two lambs didn't drink the water or eat any pellets," she said to Baba.

He looked away. "Maybe not. You'll know for sure tomorrow."

The corpses had to be removed from the pen, and quickly. Amani pointed at them.

"Can you help me carry them out? We should do it now."

Her father tensed. "I called Abu Nader, Amani. Wardeh and Raja' wanted to come and take you to school this morning. I told them you'd need this time in the pen. Abu Nader will bring his brothers to help me."

Amani shook her head. "I'm the shepherd. I should bury them."

"Not this time," Baba said. His voice broke. Amani had a feeling he'd called Mama. "Let me do this. Go to school and when you come back, you'll tend to your lambs. I'm going into Al Khalil. A friend has arranged for Mama's permit to cross the border. I'm confident she'll be home tonight with Omar."

Amani arrived at school late and sat quietly at the back

of the class. Her mind went over and over the scene at the oasis, her sheep jumping off the wall and making that fatal dash for the trough.

In English class Miss Aboushi wrote the word Ramadan on the board. Around Amani the girls bent over their desks, working on new poems. Amani stared at the white piece of paper, seeing again the stiff white backs of her sheep.

"Amani? What's wrong? Amani?" Miss Aboushi's voice grew louder.

From a great distance Amani heard her name.

Miss Aboushi knelt by her desk. All her friends stood around her. Why were they staring at her? Her teacher's question echoed in her head. What was wrong?

"My sheep."

"Yes," Miss Aboushi said, nodding. "What's happened to your sheep?"

She told them. Even Diala cried.

Amani heard a voice in her head, calling her.

Hurry.

Her chair scraped across the floor as she stood, trembling. The girls parted and she walked between them to where her coat hung on a peg.

"What's wrong, Amani?"

"I don't know. I have to go home."

TWENTY-SEVEN

AMANI DIDN'T STOP RUNNING until she reached the spot where the sidewalk met the dirt path. A few more steps made the view of the valley open up completely. She saw Seedo's Peak, directly opposite. A crowd of settlers stood behind the fence.

Her knees buckled.

On the gentle bulge at the base of Seedo's mountain most of the olive trees had been chopped down. Stumps marked the upper terraces like gravestones. Two trucks loaded with broken limbs moved west along the settlers' highway. At the bottom of the grove a digger carried and placed a small tree, root-ball intact, on a flat bed truck.

Amani cried out, wrapped her arms tightly around her stomach and kept looking.

Next to the orchard, Seedo's fig trees were all down. A big yellow backhoe was smashing apart the last standing wall of her grandfather's house. The rest was demolished, reduced to a dusty ruin. All that remained of the front porch were a few steps that led into the jagged pile of concrete blocks and rubble. Ammo Hani's house still stood on the other side of the driveway, but next in line.

The lambs.

Amani panicked, unable to see the pen. Fallen trees blocked her view. She'd left the two lambs closed off in the back of the pen. Would a bulldozer attack a small, empty sheep pen? She wanted to run and find out, but right below her, on her side of the valley, a big bulldozer rumbled toward her mother's fruit trees. Army jeeps sat parked along the shoulder of the highway. She recognized the short officer at the foot of her driveway.

The yellow Caterpillar pushed over two guava trees with its huge shovel. The cab swiveled a hundred and eighty degrees. Now the machine headed for her house, the long backhoe at its front end extended.

"Stop!" Amani screamed. Her stomach plummeted.

The heavy claw of the Caterpillar disappeared into the front of her house. Lightning cracks ripped across the roof. Dark jagged lines appeared for a split second before part of the roof caved in. White dust flew up. Out of the white cloud the yellow arm reappeared, then the Caterpillar backed up over two lemon trees. The machine crept forward to attack the next section of her house.

A flood of adrenalin roared through Amani. Think. Think. What should she do? Where was Baba? Al Khalil. She was the only family member here. Mama's piano stood by the side door. If she could stop them from demolishing the rest of her house, maybe she could save the piano.

Her knapsack felt like a burden. Amani shook it off. She imagined the wolf, the way he ran, and leapt down the mountain, sure-footed. There wasn't a second to lose. The grinding roar of the Caterpillar's engine filled her ears. Concrete dust filled her nose and mouth. She coughed, masking her face with her sleeve as she ran to the east side of her house, waving her other arm in the air.

The driver sat inside an enclosed cab. He turned his head to stare at her, spoke into something, then swiveled the Caterpillar to face her. Jumping up and down, Amani pointed to her house and back to herself. She clasped her hands together. Stop, please stop.

The huge clawed arm reached for her, coming closer. He was coming after her!

She looked down the driveway. Four soldiers were running toward her. Fast. The Caterpillar would stop if she were inside the house.

Amani took the stairs in a few bounds, turned the door-knob and pushed. The door had shifted, jammed in the frame. She threw her weight against it, hammering her body into the wood.

Strong hands caught her by the arms. In spite of her flailing, other hands grabbed her by the ankles. Four soldiers carried her down the stairs, down the driveway. She twisted violently and managed to struggle free from the soldier gripping her left ankle. She dug her heel into the ground and heard a stream of Hebrew from all four corners. Before she could squirm away, she was flipped over, pinned to the ground. She lifted her head in time to see the clawed arm reach inside the big front window of her house.

"No!" she screamed.

The wall around the window crumbled as the metal arm straightened and rose. Dust burst into a cloud. The mechanical arm rose up through the roof, and the whole front of the house collapsed.

"That's my house!"

One of the soldiers spoke Arabic. "Stay away from the house and you won't get hurt."

The attention of the soldiers shifted from the house to the highway. Amani looked, too. Along the shoulder of the road Baba charged toward them on the donkey. He was yelling, one hand waving frantically.

At the base of the driveway the officer turned to a soldier who aimed his rifle and fired.

The donkey collapsed. Baba tumbled to the ground.

"Baba!" Amani screamed.

The soldiers gripped her firmly, preventing her from running to her father.

Bleeding, the donkey lay where he'd fallen. Baba was on

his knees, trying to stand, then Amani couldn't see him for soldiers. Boots kicked. A rifle lifted. Seconds later the khaki curtain parted and she glimpsed Baba's limp body. The soldiers dragged him behind an armored vehicle. A door slammed shut.

The Caterpillar thundered past and headed across the road. The soldiers released her. Amani raised herself onto her knees. All she could think about was her father. The army vehicle holding Baba was driving away on the highway.

Amani staggered to her feet.

The soldiers didn't care what she did. They were climbing into their jeeps.

Amani limped down the driveway. They were taking Baba to a prison. She couldn't help her father right now.

There was something she still had to do. What was it?

Her lambs.

Seedo's house was demolished. Two walls of Ammo Hani's were down, and as Amani looked, a big section of the roof caved in.

The Caterpillar that had destroyed her house was heading into the olive orchard. Amani stared at the oasis. Jonathan said they wanted to move the fence lower.

If the settlers found the hidden path, what would they do to the Firdoos?

Amani crossed the highway, but instead of going up

Seedo's driveway, she crept cautiously along the shoulder of the highway.

Amma Fatima's rose garden was crushed, driven over. Amani crouched low to the ground and moved stealthily through the garden to the sheep pen. Behind a felled fig tree, the fence was knocked down. She crept over the metal gate toward the pile of wood and tin scraps where the milking pen had been that morning.

She hauled away the makeshift barrier. Two lambs huddled together beneath it. Alive. Seedo's crook lay behind them. Survivor rushed at her, the other lamb following slowly.

Amani hugged them. "Stay close. Can you do that? *Yalla.*"

Amani picked up her crook and ran from the pen. At the end of Amma Fatima's garden, near the terraces, something small and brown lay in a pool of blood by another fallen fig tree.

Amani stopped, unable to take another step.

It was Sahem. Shot.

Over the last months and hours her heart had grown harder with each new loss — a highway through their vineyards, a settlement on Seedo's Peak, Ammo Hani imprisoned, her sheep poisoned, Baba taken, their homes demolished, the olive grove destroyed. Now her heart was as heavy and full as a powder keg. The sight of Sahem struck a match. Anger exploded inside Amani, driving out fear.

There was only one thing left. The Firdoos.

Breathe, Seedo's voice said.

The lambs watched as she picked up rocks and stuffed them into her pockets.

"Stay close," she said and headed into the demolished olive grove.

On the hillside above, and ahead, the ground had already been cleared of trunks and branches. The upper terraces looked like a cemetery of scattered stumps. At the bottom of the hill two backhoes were still uprooting smaller trees. Just below Amani, the big yellow machine that had demolished her house was working alone, clearing the lower half of the hillside. Rocking on giant treads, the Caterpillar's huge metal shovel scraped across the ground, pushing an ancient tree to one side.

Amani took a rock from her pocket and aimed for the protected cab. The rock hit a corner and bounced off. But it made the driver stop and look down the slope.

Amani hurled a second rock. This time she hit a window. The driver turned. Saw Amani.

Amani threw a third rock.

The driver revved the engine. Turned the bulldozer toward her. Amani waited, shaking her crook at him. When she was sure the huge metal jaw was coming after

194

her, she turned up the hill, the lambs staying close. The machine roared.

When Amani reached the top of the hill, she turned and hurled another rock, her aim hard and true. It cracked the front window. She raised her fist. The driver shook his back at her.

Now there was no backing off for either of them. Amani drove the two lambs toward the long retaining wall. She looked back once. Yes. The huge blade followed.

She lifted the two lambs up onto the wall. They clambered over boulders, then stopped.

"Yalla!" Amani yelled.

They bent forward, jumped and disappeared. They were on the hidden path, hopefully remembering a spring and a meadow, and climbing to get there.

The Caterpillar lumbered over the oasis, coming for her.

Amani climbed onto the wall. As she did, she caught a glimpse of blue jeans — Jonathan — running down the oasis from the water trough toward them. He was waving and shouting at the driver.

There was no time to explain what she was doing, or why.

Amani threw another rock, guessing the seconds remaining between her and the enormous blade. *Six.* The driver's face was red, his mouth moving. *Five.* Perched up there in the cab, he wouldn't be able to see what the shovel smashed and crushed: the wall and, if Amani's plan did not succeed, her flesh and bones.

Amani imagined how a wolf would spring through the air.

Three…the shovel towered over her like death… *Two*…Amani turned, smelling steel…

One. Amani leapt.

TWENTY-EIGHT

THE LEAP DIDN'T GO EXACTLY as planned. She did not bound over the second boulder, but landed on it. Briefly. She sprang off, hurtling up the path. Her heels barely touched the ground.

Behind her, the ground shuddered violently. Amani kept running, putting distance between herself, the Caterpillar and a possible landslide.

She glanced back. Exploding rocks. Dust. A hill of boulders sliding.

Terrified, she flew up the path, running, running until she disappeared around the edge of the Camel's Hump.

Was she far enough yet? Yes. She peered back. The dust and the Caterpillar were gone from view. Immediately she slowed her pace, leaning heavily on Seedo's crook, gasping for breath.

It wasn't long before she caught up with the two lambs. The weak one had stopped, unable to continue. Survivor was nudging it, bleating at it.

Amani scooped the lamb under one arm. It was seven

months old, big enough to be awkward. Amani had to switch the lamb from one aching arm to the other before she finally reached the flat ground of the plateau.

She eyed the plateau, wondering if she had the strength to make it to the Firdoos. She slung the weak lamb over her shoulders. She leaned on her shepherd's crook. The olive wood was warm under her fingers. She walked slowly, grateful Survivor was able to move by herself.

The rocky stairway was a challenge. She took it one step at a time, placing the crook above her and pulling herself up. Resting a few breaths before she attempted the next. Then the meadow opened before her, green and sun-drenched. High up the slope she spotted the wolf with his family.

Survivor ran to the stream and Amani let her, wondering what the wolves would do. They watched. Waited.

Amani walked to the stream and set the weak lamb beside the water, hoping it might at least drink. It didn't.

Overcome by thirst, Amani knelt on the ground and prayed *Bism Allah al-rahman al-raheem*. She washed her right hand, her left, and then drank. Cold, sweet and fresh, the water revived her. She drank and drank until Survivor, oblivious to everything but her hunger, headed into the meadow to eat.

Amani followed. She let Survivor eat as long as she

dared. She turned away from the weak lamb by the stream and stared up at the wolves.

"I leave you one," she said, and drove Survivor off the meadow.

TWENTY-NINE

AMANI ROUNDED THE CAMEL'S HUMP and began the descent through the boulders. The sun was a small red ember on the western horizon. Survivor stuck to her heels, nearly tripping her when she stopped. The way ahead was blocked where boulders had shifted and resettled after the bulldozer's attack.

Amani estimated she'd have to climb twenty meters down over the boulders to reach the wall. Would it be safe?

A lumpy shadow occupied a piece of ground on the oasis below her. A long shape, possibly a rifle, lay on the ground beside it.

A settler?

Cautious and quiet, Amani climbed onto the boulders with Survivor. The shape didn't move.

She descended carefully, stepping from the middle of one boulder to the next, relieved when it didn't move, when the lumpy shadow didn't, either. She stopped when she stood on the pile of rubble that had been the retaining wall.

The shadow was Jonathan. He was sitting cross-legged, hunched forward, like someone who'd waited a long time in the damp chill and fallen asleep.

She was very glad to see him.

"Jonathan!"

He straightened. Groaned. Jumped to his feet.

"Oh, my God," he said, walking toward her. "Palestine. You're alive."

Using her crook to steady herself on the broken rocks, Amani climbed down and out of the mess. Jonathan reached out a hand to help, smiling like crazy.

"I kept praying you'd made it up the path. I couldn't see for the dust. Why did you do that?"

"My grandfather was a shepherd," she said. "He kept that path a secret. I had to do the same. Do the settlers know about it?"

"Only me."

"Then they won't find it easily."

He pulled her toward the long, bulky bundle. He had to let go of her hand to pick it up, and though she was sorry, she was relieved, too.

"I brought you a blanket. Can you carry your lamb? There's still poison around. Where do you want to go?"

"Are they watching?"

He shook his head. "They're celebrating."

They walked in silence where the olive terraces had

been. It was almost dark. Diesel fumes still clung to the ground. The hillside was bare except for stumps where trees had been chopped down instead of uprooted. There was no garden, no path, yet Amani's feet knew the way.

A whiff of musty rock made Amani laugh. The cave! The home of her ancestors hadn't been demolished. Finding the cave felt like a small blessing. Then she tripped over something and fell.

"Are you okay?" Jonathan switched on a flashlight, circling the beam of light until it found her.

Amani stared at Sitti's bake-oven beside her.

"It's still here," she whispered. "My grandmother will be glad. Should you turn off the light?"

"We're hidden by the hill," he said "I think it's safe to build a fire. I brought food."

The mention of food reminded Amani that she hadn't eaten all day, maybe longer. She was ravenous. But there was something she had to do first.

"Can I use your light?"

He passed it to her. She went into the cave and brought back a shovel.

Jonathan helped her bury Sahem. It didn't take long and she was glad to have Jonathan's silent company, glad when it was done.

They gathered wood and soon sat on two broken chairs in front of a glowing fire, eating fellafel. Jonathan opened the top of a carton, poured liquid into his upturned mouth, then handed Amani the carton.

"Cheers. Chocolate milk."

She drank the thick sweet liquid. Not as good as spring water, she thought, but delicious because he'd thought to bring it.

"Where's your family?" he asked.

She told him. "I'll sleep in the cave tonight. When it's light, I'll go to the village. Then I have to find my father."

He stared into the flames, breaking sticks between his hands. He tossed one after another into the fire.

"I'm going back to New York."

She didn't want him to go.

"Why? Are you a coward?"

He flinched. "My father called me that. He says a real Jew defends the Holy Land. I don't know what a real Jew is anymore. My grandparents saw so many Jews die in the camps. They believed in a homeland where Jews would be safe, but I can't believe they meant this." He shook his head. "When I saw that bulldozer going after you..." His voice broke.

Amani remembered how he'd run to stop the bulldozer. He'd sat in the cold on the oasis until she returned. If all the settlers were more like Jonathan and that rabbi Baba knew, they'd be able to work out a solution.

"You are not a coward," she said. "I said it because I don't want you to go. I am afraid of the settlers. I'm not so afraid if I know you are there."

"I can't stay in the settlement. Every day I think how your life must have been before. I imagine you grazing your sheep like that first day I saw you. No fences. No soldiers. No highways over your land. The settlement destroyed your life. Going back to New York I can talk about you, about what I've seen. You'll have to imagine me in New York."

He kept staring at her. "You are the most amazing girl I'll ever meet. I wish…I wish so many things."

She wished she could tell him how much she liked him.

"When will you leave?"

"Tomorrow. I'd stay with you tonight, but if I don't get back to the settlement soon, they'll think you've killed me and send the army to search the village."

"I am safe in the cave. My grandfather slept here with his sheep when he was a boy. Thank you for the blanket and the food." Amani stared at his face, knowing she had to memorize it quickly. "Do you want to know something, before you go?"

The eagerness in his eyes made her heart snap the picture. That was how she'd remember him. Long hair over his ears, his wide smile, his broad shoulders leaning forward.

"My name, Amani, means wishes, but I have only one," she began.

And a billion stars listened as Amani recited for Jonathan the poem she wrote in English class, the story of her birth.

THIRTY

CUDDLED NEXT TO THE WARM WEIGHT of her lamb, Amani woke up, smiling. Music. She was sure she heard music.

She opened her eyes to silence.

Usually the call to prayer woke her. Was that what she'd heard? It sounded more like a piano.

She flung off the blanket and stood up, confused. She was in the dark mouth of the cave. Waking from a wonderful dream of Mama playing the piano.

The light of day snapped her back into reality.

In front of her lay the ruins of Seedo's house, the broken limbs of fruit trees, everything covered in white concrete dust. On the other side of the highway her house was much the same: a ragged pile of broken concrete blocks.

Survivor bleated at her, hungry and thirsty. Amani found a pail and filled it at the well. Then she crossed the highway with the lamb, heading for a bit of green.

"Amani!" a voice shouted from inside her demolished house. She looked at the vaguely rectangular shape. One end was higher than the other.

Was that a head poking out from the middle? A hand waving?

"Amani!"

The head disappeared for a second and then emerged from another spot inside the crumbled house. Two people were hatching out of the broken shell of her house. A woman, head bent, climbed carefully between the pieces of fallen roof. Amani recognized the blonde streak of hair.

"Mama!" Amani shouted, running toward them. "Omar!"

They met on the shoulder of the settlers' highway. Arms wrapped around each other, they swayed together, a small circle of three. They cried, even Omar. Amani kissed her mother, her brother, over and over, staring at their faces in disbelief.

"When did you get back?" Amani asked.

They broke apart to wipe their eyes. Mama was crying too much to finish a sentence.

"Yesterday afternoon," Omar said. "Half the village came with us. We were just in time to see them take a truckload of trees to sell in Tel Aviv. A soldier told us Baba attacked the army on his donkey and that he was taken away. He said a girl with two sheep — "

Omar gripped Amani's wrists, still tender from yesterday, and she cried out, "Aiee! You're hurting!"

He let go. "He said you went crazy and attacked a bull-dozer. He said you were probably dead."

Mama sobbed. "Someone found your knapsack on the mountain path. Islah made us come back to the village. I couldn't sleep for worry. Where have you been?"

"I'm sorry, Mama. I hid with the lambs in the hills. Then it was dark and it felt safer to sleep in the cave than try to get into the village."

Mama reached out her arms and they hugged. "You did the right thing."

Amani remembered her confusion waking up and pulled away. "I woke up hearing music. Mama, did I hear you playing the piano?"

Mama wiped her eyes and laughed. She pointed to the high end of their demolished house. "We were looking for you. A big slab of the roof landed on top of the hallway by the side door. It's amazing how the bulldozer missed it. Everything on both sides of the hallway is smashed. It looks like the bulldozer was blocked by the stairway in front of the door."

"Baba said we needed the piano to bring you home."

"And it did! Look at me! I'm home. I'll never leave the valley again."

Amani began to cry again as she told them what had happened to Baba.

"The soldiers took him away just like Ammo Hani. I

think we should call Baba's Israeli and international friends. That's what Baba did when Ammo Hani was taken."

"How can we?" Mama asked.

"If we find his little book of names and phone numbers, we could — "

"I have friends in Ramallah," Omar said loudly. "There are other ways to demand the release of prisoners."

Amani read his eyes. He meant violence. She recognized the anger inside her brother.

"Those ways are a death sentence for all of us," Mama said, shaking her head.

They were heading for a fight. Amani tried to calm them.

"This doesn't help Baba. Where did he keep his address book? We should call his friends. Then I'm going to the prison. That's what Baba did. Will you take me, Omar?"

Her brother nodded grudgingly. "He kept the book in his desk. I'll go look."

"Sometimes he kept it in a coat pocket," Mama said, walking toward the house with him.

Survivor bleated. The lamb had wandered away, searching for food. A car drove by. Amani couldn't leave the lamb alone so close to the road. She walked toward her on the shoulder of the highway.

Suddenly Amani felt prickles at the back of her neck.

She was nearing the spot where she'd last seen Baba. Someone had taken the donkey's body away, but a dark stain of blood on the crushed stones in front of her made Amani fall to her hands and knees.

With her fingers she felt over the stones. Something was here. The dirt filled her nails but she crawled over the spot, searching. Her fingertips touched something smooth, metallic. She held it in her palm and brushed the dirt away.

Amani spat on Baba's cellphone, rubbed it clean with the inside edge of her shirt and pressed the tiny spot. It flicked open.

Which key next? She'd watched Baba do this a hundred times. She pressed the key at the top left. The screen lit up. Menu. Address book. A list of names. She read them carefully.

She pressed a highlighted name. A number filled the screen. She pressed again. Heard the rhythmic ring. A click.

"*Shalom…*" A man's voice. She didn't understand what he said.

"Hello," Amani said loudly in English. "My name is Amani Raheem. I think you know my father. I think you are a friend."

The man switched to English. "Raheem? Are you Aref's daughter?"

"Yes, rabbi. Soldiers came. They broke our house. They took my father. Can you help me find him?"

The man spoke slowly for Amani, unfamiliar words she tried to repeat in her head, especially one. They said good-bye.

Amani picked up Survivor and ran to the house to tell Mama and Omar.

"The rabbi's coming," she explained. "Baba's friend. He's coming to help us."

"A rabbi?" Mama's eyes widened.

"He promised he'd come today. He doesn't think we should go to the prison. He has a plan."

"You're asking us to trust a rabbi?" Omar's face said he could never do it.

"Yes. He wants us to wait here. He's calling other friends. He hopes to bring," she wished the rabbi had repeated the strange word, "an Israeli low-cee-er."

Omar shook his fist. It was the same gesture Ammo Hani used to make. "No! We'll get a Palestinian lawyer if we need one. What do you know about the world, Amani? Nothing. It's a stupid idea, asking Israelis for help."

He turned away, kicking loose rocks as he headed back to the house.

"Give him time, Amani," Mama said. "He's had a long week of worrying and being searched and detained at checkpoints. If these men prove to be friends as you say, he'll come around. Let's see what we can save from the house."

Starting at one end of the house they worked through the rubble, salvaging anything they could. A few pots and dishes were unbroken in a cupboard. Towels. Clothing from broken dressers. The space heater had been stored in a cupboard and was thankfully in one piece. Amani found and dragged out several mattresses in reasonable condition.

Without speaking or making eye contact, Omar came to help her. They took turns, one trying to hold the big wobbly cushion steady while the other beat it with a broom. Amani kept her face as stony as her brother's. Concrete dust loosened and flew away, and suddenly Amani heard Seedo's old words — *Sweep it from your heart.*

Amani peeked at her brother swinging the broom. She let go of the mattress just before he struck. It flopped over, and Omar onto it.

"You're in for it now!" He yelled, rolling to his feet.

Amani grinned, pointing at him. "You've aged in Ramallah. Your hair's as white as Seedo's."

His eyes were two round holes in a powdery face until his mouth opened to make a third. He smiled at her.

"Like it? Think I look good old? Want to look good, too? Want to look like Sitti?"

Oh, oh. She knew that smile. She turned to run but he

caught her, and was about to toss her onto the dusty mattress when a long white van drove off the highway, tooting its horn.

Omar dropped her. The van parked in front of the blockade at the bottom of the driveway. Omar brushed the dust from his face and clothes, moving toward it. Four doors opened and six people climbed out. The driver wore a red baseball cap and waved cheerfully. From the back of the van they began to unload boxes. Someone carried two potted olive saplings over to Omar.

"Are you the man in charge?"

Omar nodded.

"Where do you want these?"

Pointing to the empty terraces on the other side of the highway, Omar said, "Follow me. I'll find a shovel."

THIRTY-ONE

IT WAS ALMOST DARK WHEN a dented silver car with yellow license plates parked where the van had sat all afternoon before leaving. Omar strode down the driveway to confront the man wearing a circle hat, and his passenger, a woman wearing a dark pantsuit. Amani ran to catch up with Omar, worried how he'd receive the new visitors. She recognized the tall rabbi with curly brown hair, smiling at Omar. Omar didn't smile back.

Amani extended a quick hand.

"Ahlan."

The rabbi shook her hand. "You must be Amani, the one who called? I remember you from the protest. Let me tell you what's happened. We stopped at the jail inside the settlement. That's where they took him. We saw your father." The rabbi spoke excellent Arabic with a heavy American accent.

The message and accent sounded just like Miss Aboushi. Omar's hard expression cracked open a little.

"You saw my father?" he asked.

The rabbi nodded and introduced the lawyer, who

didn't speak much Arabic. They switched to English. The lawyer explained that she'd arranged a hearing for early the next morning.

"We have to act before he's sent to another prison or dumped beyond the border. If that happens, coming home becomes impossible. It's all done to discourage your resistance." She gave Amani a look full of warmth and admiration. "You were very smart to act so quickly. And your English is exceptional."

Amani blushed.

"How is he?" Omar asked.

"Not too bad," the rabbi answered. "Some broken ribs but he's in good spirits. Very pleased to have a lawyer."

"Will they free him?"

"It will depend on the allegations against him," the lawyer said. "But he had no weapons. He was alone. A man hurrying toward his house that is suddenly being demolished is only guilty of hurrying toward his house."

The rabbi nodded. "If God is in the courtroom tomorrow, and no settlers show up, she might persuade the judge he was innocent. But your father organized a protest. Being a leader makes him a target. Worse, you have land and water beside the new settlement. I'm sorry they demolished your homes and dug up your olives. If we'd been here, we might have been able to stop them. Sometimes we can."

Mama nudged Omar for a translation. While he translated, Amani stared at the lawyer. Her gray hair made her look older than Mama, but her skin was clear and youthful. Amani admired her air of authority and intelligence. She wished she could go to the courtroom tomorrow and hear her argue.

"Ahlan," Mama said. "You will be our guests. One of the Christian peacemakers is staying, too. We haven't eaten and there's plenty to go around, *Insha'allah*. It's easier to talk when your stomach isn't grumbling."

They nodded gratefully. Below the demolished house a big canvas tent donated by the International Red Cross had been erected during the afternoon. Amani found and lit two kerosene lamps and a heater while Omar helped the man in the red baseball cap close the flaps. They huddled in a tight circle around the evening meal.

Amani sat beside Omar, hardly able to eat, stealing glances at the guests sharing their food. They seemed to know each other well and chatted as they dipped into the bowls of food. They praised Mama's cooking, and when Omar translated their comments, she blushed like a girl.

Omar asked many questions. The Christian was from the United States. The rabbi was from Jerusalem. The lawyer lived in Tel Aviv and worked for human rights. Baba had met them when he'd organized the mobile clinic and the protest against the highway.

"So you work together?"

They looked at each other and laughed.

"Sometimes. We try. God would be very happy if we did."

"Did you try to free my uncle?"

"We did. We're still trying."

"Can you help us rebuild our house?"

"You can't do anything without a permit. Without a permit they'll come and demolish anything you build."

"How do we get a permit?"

"It's expensive. We'll try to raise money for you."

Omar turned quiet when they said that.

Amani cleared her throat. The lawyer noticed.

"Yes, Amani?"

"What's happened to our muezzin? There hasn't been a call to prayer for two days."

The three guests exchanged a long look. The rabbi answered. "The soldiers have probably ordered it stopped. They say it disturbs their sleep."

The lawyer quickly suggested it was a good time for them to sleep. She needed to have her wits about her for the hearing. They spread out the mattresses smelling of concrete dust. Amani didn't mind, grateful to be off the cold ground. Twice during the night someone got up to tie the tent flaps a little tighter. Winter crept under the canvas walls. Amani burrowed deeper under her blankets,

Survivor warm on her feet, surrounded by friends and family.

After breakfast the guests said goodbye. Mama was frustrated that she couldn't speak their language. There was so much she wanted to say to them.

Omar and Amani were walking their guests to their car when the piano music began. They were enchanted, and when Omar told them how the piano survived the demolition, they were amazed.

"Now, that's a miracle," the Christian peacemaker said, and whistled.

THIRTY-TWO

"THINK ABOUT IT," Miss Aboushi said.

The most incredible teacher in the world had walked down the mountain to visit them. When she left, the real reason turned out to be a thin package she handed to Amani.

"There's a school in Ramallah that has a good international program. I know some of the teachers. It would be a wonderful high school for you next year."

"I can't leave the valley, Miss Aboushi. I'm a shepherd."

"I know you're a shepherd. Read the brochure. Promise me you'll think about it."

Abu Nader also dropped by. He, too, had an offer. He wanted to give Amani his ram, Surprise, and his last remaining lamb so that she could build a new flock. He only had one condition. Every spring for the next four years she had to give him a lamb.

Amani remembered how good Seedo had been at bartering, and immediately said four was too many. He came down to three.

"Give me a little time to think about it," Amani said.

219

In the afternoon Amani took Survivor to graze the slope above her house. She walked for a long time until she was ready to be still and think. She sat where she had a good view of the valley. A last group of villagers dropped by to inspect the tent and drink tea.

Amani read the brochure twice, then tried to imagine leaving the valley.

Survivor rested at her feet. Amani patted the black head, admiring the lamb's long eyelashes.

"You had the most wonderful grandmother. Next summer you may have twins to keep you happy, *Insha'allah*. You wouldn't miss me. A shepherd needs sheep. Sheep need land to graze, and it's getting complicated. Abu Nader could take care of you."

The western sky beyond the village turned orange and purple.

Across the valley lay the ruins of Ammo Hani's and Seedo's houses. It hurt to look at them, and at the empty hillside below the oasis. Relatives and neighbors had come by all day, promising to help rebuild the stone terraces for a new olive orchard. The roots of two new saplings, gifts from the peacemakers, were already reaching into the soil.

Her valley, her home.

The sound of a car on the settler's highway made Amani look west.

Headlights. The car slowed, the hum of tires becoming

a soft crunch on the tiny stones of the shoulder. The car stopped by the blockade below the tent.

Amani stood. The headlights of the dented, silvery car went out. Doors opened and slammed shut.

Helped by two friends, a man on crutches looked up at Amani and waved.

Amani lifted her head and ululated, the long trill in her throat a song of welcome for a loved one returning home.

GLOSSARY

Ahlan: Welcome

Aliya: Immigrating to Israel (Hebrew for ascending)

Al Khalil: Hebron

Allah: God

Allahu Akbar: God is great

Al Nakba: The catastrophe of 1948

'Amma: Aunt

'Ammo: Uncle on father's side

Bar mitzvah: Hebrew term for coming of age

Bism Allah al-rahman al-raheem: In the Name of God the Most Kind the Most Merciful

Fellafel: Deep-fried balls of ground chickpeas

Ghummayeh: Hide-and-seek

Habeebi/habibti: Darling

Haeretz: Land of Israel (Hebrew); literally the land

Hawiyyeh: Identification papers

Hijab: Woman's headscarf

Insha'allah: God willing

Intifada: Uprising, shaking off

Keefik: How are you? (addressing one female person)

Khalas: Enough

Kufiyyi: Man's traditional headscarf

Kul yom: Every day

Lasamahallah: God forbid

Marhaba: Welcome

Mossad: Israeli Intelligence (Hebrew)

Muezzin: Person who calls to the Islamic congregational prayer, often from the minaret of a mosque

Qur'an: Holy Book of Islam

Rouh: Go

Sahem/Sahm: Arrow

Salam: Peace

Shalom: Peace (Hebrew)

Shin Bet: Israel's internal security service

Shrak: Thin wholewheat bread baked over a domed griddle

Tawjihi: Secondary school examination in the West Bank, Gaza and Jordan

Yalla: Let's go

Za'tar: Dried thyme, crushed into a powder.

Zaytoon: Olives

ANNE LAUREL CARTER is an award-winning author of books for children and young people. Since 1971 she has visited Israel several times, working on kibbutzim and studying Hebrew, as well as teaching in Ramallah, where she stayed with several Palestinian families while researching this novel. Her young adult novel *Last Chance Bay* won the Canadian Library Association Book of the Year Award, and her picture book *Under a Prairie Sky* (illustrated by Alan and Lea Daniel) won the Mr. Christie's Book Award.

Anne is a teacher-librarian in Toronto.